Arthur Sketchley

Mrs. Brown on the Royal Russian Marriage

Arthur Sketchley

Mrs. Brown on the Royal Russian Marriage

ISBN/EAN: 9783337298951

Printed in Europe, USA, Canada, Australia, Japan

Cover: Foto ©Andreas Hilbeck / pixelio.de

More available books at **www.hansebooks.com**

Mrs. Brown on the Royal Russian Marriage.

BY

ARTHUR SKETCHLEY,

AUTHOR OF "THE BROWN PAPERS."

LONDON:

GEORGE ROUTLEDGE AND SONS,

THE BROADWAY, LUDGATE.

MRS. BROWN ON THE ROYAL RUSSIAN MARRIAGE.

PREFACE.

"WELL," I says to Miss Pilkinton, "let 'im marry
a Rooshun if he likes, jest the same as 'is sister did
a Prooshun, for there ain't 'ardly a pin to choose
between 'em; and, for my part, if he were a son
of mine, and 'is 'art in the 'Ighlands, as the sayin'
is, I should be better pleased, jest like 'is other
sister as is married to that there young Scotch lord,
and as 'appy as the day is long, and quite used to
'im a-goin' about the 'ouse with no trousers on, as
no doubt give 'er a turn at fust. But he's a werry
nice young man, and looks werry well in them outlandish togs, as I see 'im a-dancin' in myself thro'
a-bein' over in Scotland myself this 'ere last fall;
and I'm sure it's to be 'oped as the Duke of Edinburer won't dress up for a Scotchman over in
Roosher, as the cold would be sure to strike to 'im

with nothink but a kilt on, as it's wonderful as they can go about them 'ills with no more on in Scotland."

Tho' I do 'ope as Roosher ain't so dull as that there Inwerary, as' they calls it, as is where that there young Lord lives along with 'is Princess, and 'is father and mother too, as ain't a good plan in my opinion, cos it's best when young people starts in life as they should be left to theirselves, cos, tho' in course that Dook and Duchess knows their place too well for to talk that free with a Princess, tho' she is their son's wife; yet it must be unpleasant for 'er to 'ave to order them about, and for them to 'ave to knock under to 'er, cos, in course, they're nobodies when she's by; and of all the dismal 'oles as ever I did see it's the kirk as she've got to go to of a Sunday, as is a reglar rookery, as is a thing as this 'ere Rooshun Princess won't stand, for I've see a Rooshun church over in Paris as is awful grand, and tho' they're a topsy-turvey sort of religion, them Rooshuns, yet don't give you the 'orrers like them dismal, 'owlin' Scotch. As for my part, I'd rather be no religion at all, cos wotever is the use on it if it ain't a comfort to you, as I'm sure that kirk never would be to me.

But, as I says, let parties do as they likes, and if they're pleased I'm sure I am.

But wot puzzles me is 'owever that there Dook of

Edinburer ever come to see that there Rooshun young lady, tho' it's werry often the way, partikler in plays and story-books, the same as Romulus and Julio, as was deadly henemies jest like us and the Rooshuns, and so their parents wouldn't 'ear on it; but wotever were the use of opposin' it, as only ended unpleasant thro' both on 'em a-pisonin' of theirselves, and I don't believe as Queen Wictoria would ever 'ave the 'art to be that flinty, and in course if she did say no would stick to it, but wouldn't never forgive 'erself if they were to take and swaller pison, or be found drownded, or any other wiolent death, tho' a fine thing for the papers.

Miss Pilkinton she will 'ave it as it ain't lorful thro' 'er not bein' the 'Stablished Church, and don't keep Christmas-day the same as us, nor yet Easter; but no doubt she'll give in to 'is way, tho' 'er old father is a bit of a Tartar I've 'eard say over religion, and reglar bullies 'is bishops.

But he knows too well which side 'is bread is buttered, not to ketch at one of Queen Wictorier's sons for a 'usban' for 'is dorter, and will eat 'umble pie over Christmas along with 'is plum-puddin'.

Miss Pilkinton she says he's a growin' power, as will overrun us all some day.

I says, "Let 'im grow, in welcome; but as to runnin' over us, if he tries that on we shall soon pull 'im up."

"Well," says Miss Pilkinton, "I 'ope it may end well, but I don't seem to fancy keepin' of two Christmas-days in one family."

"Well," I says, "it's certingly bad for the children, tho' I 'ave knowed families as kep' New Year's-day jest like Christmas, and 'ad two family parties thro' bein' two grandfathers and grand-mothers; but," I says, "in course we knows as there can only be but one proper Christmas-day, as only comes but once a year, as the sayin' is, tho' I certingly knowed a party as kep' two in one year, and all thro' bein' in the seafarin' line and a sailin' to Roosher, and so 'ad two Christmas-days—one with the Rooshuns and the other like Christians, cos them Rooshuns not a-believin' in the Pope won't 'ave 'is Christmas-day, as is the same as wot the Inglish keeps, and that's 'ow it is as they differs with the Scotch, as 'ates the Pope, and won't 'ave no Christmas at all, as is wot I calls a-cuttin' off your nose to be rewenged on your face, as the sayin' is; and reglar poor spite, cos wotever does the Pope care whether they keeps Christmas or not, as eats 'is roast beef and plum-puddin' no doubt all the same, and don't bother his head over the Scotch, as is werry strict over keepin' New Year's day, for there ain't 'ardly a man, woman, or child in all Scotland as is sober then from morning till night, as shows their 'igh sperrit in doin' wot they likes, and don't pay no attention to the Pope nor nobody else as tries to check 'em."

So I says to Mrs. McCullum, as were a-tellin' me as the Pope were anti-crust, and kep' a-goin' on about 'im bein' the man of sin, till I says to her, " Why, any one would think, to 'ear you run 'im down, as he were a teatotaler," for she liked a drop 'ot and strong of a night, partikler the Sabbath, as I think the cold dinner and two long sermons give 'er a chill, and no wonder, for I'm sure I couldn't stand neither myself; but, as I always says, let parties do as they likes with their meals and their church, so as they don't force neither their cold dinners nor long sermons on me.

But 'owever parties can get on without Christmas I can't think, as it wouldn't seem to me like 'uman nature if it didn't come round. Besides, 'owever should we know when it was the New Year if it didn't come the week after Christmas.

And then I do like a-makin' of my mincemeat and my puddin's, cos I always makes mine a pound-puddin', as I diwides into three, not as I wants to eat it all myself, but there's plenty of mouths as is ready for a bit, as preaps 'ave made a 'eavy 'eart cheer up of a Christmas-day at the werry name on it, the same as poor Emly Thrupley, as certingly did be'ave foolish but not bad, and certingly not enuf to make 'er own father cuss 'er as he did to

my werry face, and more to be pitied than blamed,
for she 'adn't no mother, and he was a 'ard man
was Thrupley, and belonged to a chapel up the
City Road way, as said they was the werry elect,
and nobody couldn't be saved out of it; so he
walked to it twice every Sunday, that he did, winter
and summer, and would try and drag that poor boy
along with 'im; and to 'ear 'im go on about
Christmas bein' 'eathen ways, was aggrawatin'

Till I says to 'im one day on my own doorstep,
the week before Christmas, as I was a-takin' in my
groceries, I says, "Who are you a-callin' of a
'eathen, as was christened under the month, and
knowed my catechism down to the sacraments afore
I got married, so don't you talk about 'eathens;
and as to your a-darin' to say as you're right and
nobody else, why, it's downright worse than 'eathen,
for it's impidence; and as to your minister, as no
doubt gets a werry nice little livin' out of his chapel,
why, I don't consider 'im no better than the Punch
and Judy man, as shows it for the coppers as he
can pick up at it."

I says, "You may call me a Malickite or
Caninite, but I considers you no better than
a Bedlamite; so don't you come none of your impidence over Christmas to me, as knows my dooty,
and I 'opes tries to do it, Christmas or no Christmas,
as I means to keep to my dyin' day."

Not as I should like to live over in Horsetralier, where they keeps it at Midsummer with a pic-nic, as must be jest for the sake of bein' contrary, like the 'Merrykins; but as to goin' out into the country, and a-settin' on the grass, with cold lamb and salid, on Christmas-day, I'd as soon think of 'avin' 'ot roast beef and plum-puddin' in the dog-days, when you can't fancy butcher's meat.

But, as I were a-sayin', poor Emly Thrupley she 'adn't no sich a life on it at 'ome, partikler arter 'er mother's death; and the boy, he run away to sea thro' not bein' able for to stand 'is father and the chapel no longer, thro' both children a-sidin' with the mother, as were the Hirish way of thinkin'

I must say as I were werry angry with Emly when she come to me in 'er trouble jest before 'er baby were born, and said as she'd been married on the sly to that young Ryan as were in the theatrical line, and 'er father wouldn't never 'ear on cos of the religion.

I says to her, I says, " Emly, you ain't no longer a hinfant in the eye of the law, as the sayin' is, thro' bein' one-and-twenty two year ago; but," I says, "a-goin and marryin' on the sly ain't actin' by a parent over and above board, tho' I must say as your father is enuf to prowoke a saint."

" Well," she says, "my 'usban' 'as got a 'ome for me all ready, and I'm a-goin' to it now."

"Well, then," I says, "go to it, as is your dooty to, thro' 'avin' sworn it at the halter; and you'd better rite to your father, or, if you like, I'll go and tell 'im," for I'd knowed 'im since afore she was born.

"Oh!" she says, "if you would, Mrs. Brown, I'd thank you on my bended knees."

I says, "There ain't no occasions for no bended knees; but," I says, "rite to 'im, and I'll go and see 'im jest arter he's got the letter, as you 'ad better leave on the table with 'is tea."

"Oh!" she says, "he always gets that for 'isself, and won't trust me to make it."

I says, "Then leave the letter on the table, and I'll drop in permiscuous like, jest arter five, and I'll come and see you by and by," cos she'd give me 'er address, as were close by, where she were a-goin' to live with 'er 'usban', as were only six months between 'em.

I 'ave seen parties in rages, and see the devil in their faces, but never nothink like old Thrupley, as were 'avin' 'is tea when I went in, and says quite short, "I suppose you've come to say as my dorter's gone somewhere's a-pleasurin'; but if it's a theayter, she may stop there for ever, for I won't 'ave 'er under my roof no more."

I says, "You're a nice father, you are, as would like your dorter to stop for ever in a place as you considers bad; but," I says, "I suppose you ain't read 'er letter?"

"No," he says, "and don't want to read it. I told 'er if ever she entered the doors of a theayter I'd never see 'er no more."

"Ah!" I says, "no doubt theayters is bad places, and I'm sure I wonders as many on 'em don't get their deaths of cold in them, a-standin' about as they do with 'ardly nothink on; but," I says, "I don't think as she gone to no theayter— leastways I'm sure she ain't, tho' she might go to wuss, for I 'ave knowed them as got no good thro' goin' to chapel; for," I says, "actors ain't the wust men as I've 'eard on, nor yet actresses neither, cos," I says, "I've knowed ministers do wuss things than ever actors 'as done; and, I can tell you, I've knowed actors as 'ave shared their bit of grub with one another, when there wasn't much to share neither, for they was all pretty near a-starvin' together down in the country near Liza's; and I only 'opes that's wot all ministers does, as in course bein' that good don't care wot they eats or drinks, or where they lives, so long as they can be a-doin' good."

He didn't say nothink, but kep' on at 'is tea, as I let 'im finish; not as he asked me to take a cup, as I shouldn't 'ave took, thro' 'avin' 'ad mine 'arf a 'our afore.

So he only groaned at me, a-praisin' play-actors with 'is mouth full of creases, and when he'd done, he gets up and takes up the tea tray, and there was Emly's letter a-layin' on the table, leastways 'ad stuck to the bottom of the tray, but fell of in 'im a-liftin' of it up.

He put the tea tray on the dresser, and picks up the letter as he opened and read; and 'adn't no sooner done it than he give a rush at me, and shook me wiolent by the shoulder.

I says, " Stand off, you little ottomy, do," and took and give 'im a shove as sent a-reelin' back'ards into 'is chair.

" Oh ! " he says, a-glarin' at me, and a-shakin' of both 'is fists at me ; " this is your wile works."

I says, " Bless the man. Me, indeed, I never rote to you."

He says, " No," but he says, " you've been at the bottom of this."

I says, " I ain't been at the bottom nor the top of nothink, if you're illudin' to your dorter's letter, 'cos I never 'eard a word on it till about a 'our ago, when she come and told me."

He read that letter over agin, and then says, ' Who is he ? Who is the willin ? "

I says, " I never set eyes on 'im, but am told as 'is name is Ryan."

He says, " Ryan ! then he is a wile stage play-actor, the feller as I desired 'er never to see agin."

If he didn't go to the shelf and bring out 'is Bible and open it, as I thought he were a-goin' to read it for to comfort 'im ; but he took and opened it, and a-layin' 'is 'and on it, and 'is face blue with rage, begun for to let out the cusses over 'is child, as made my blood run cold.

So I gives a dash at the Bible, and snatches it away, and says, " Cuss away, you wild old reprerbate, do ; but don't dare for to insult this 'oly book by a-puttin' your 'and on it with sich words as them in your mouth."

He says, " Give me that book."

I says, " Never, for to see you treat it like that, as would sooner throw it on the fire fust ; so," I says, " you may come and fetch it, and cuss over it when I'm gone, but never shall in my presence."

So I walks out and puts the Bible down on a ledge, as is jest inside of the street door ; and 'ome I went, and then on to poor Emly's, to tell 'er about 'er father.

She was a-settin' with 'er 'usban', as were jest a-goin' out, as nice a lookin' young feller as you'd wish to see, but far from strong ; as told me he were in the purfession, a-meanin' the stage, and were a-gettin' on werry nicely.

" Well," I says, " only take care of yourself, for

them theayters is terrible drafty places, and the late 'ours, with all that gas is werry tryin' "

He says as it were so, and 'adn't no time to stay any longer, as he were on at seven, so said good by, and give Emly a kiss, and were off.

I says, " My dear, he ain't strong, so mind as you 'ave 'is bit of supper all ready for 'im at night when he comes in, so as he may 'ave a object for to 'urry 'ome to."

We was a-talkin' all about 'erself when the door bust open, and in walks old Thrupley.

" Father," says Emly, a-'oldin' out 'er arms.

He give 'er a orful scowl, and says, " Stand back, you wile, wicked, may the cuss ——"

I didn't 'ear no more, but I took and give a spring at 'im, seized 'im by the throat, and shoved my pocket 'ankercher into 'is mouth till he 'eaved agin, for I see as the poor gal 'ad turned dead faint, and dropped into a chair.

I forced the old willin into the passage, and I says to 'im, " If you dares to say one word like that to your own child, I'll strangle you if I'm 'ung for it ; " and I took and shoved 'im out at the street door into the street, as he'd left open.

When I went back to that poor gal she was in sterrics, and I never left her for a minit till 'er 'usban' came in from the theayter, as went for a party as she'd engaged to nuss 'er, and afore ever

Mr. Bolus come the child was born, as were a reglar little waxwork model of a gal.

I didn't get 'ome till jest on three, as didn't matter thro' Brown bein' away, but a bitter cold night jest two days afore Christmas.

Both mother and child was a-doin' well on Christmas-day, as the weather 'ad turned right down muggy, so I thought as I'd 'ave a try for to soften down old Thrupley, as I knowed wouldn't be at chapel, 'cos he don't believe in Christmas, nor none of its blessin's, so was a whitewashin' 'is front kitchen.

I ketched 'im a-standin' on the steps, with the top of the kitchen winder open, but he turns on me like a green dragon as I spoke to 'im thro' it, and says, "Don't you come 'ere, or I shall do you a mischief."

"Oh!" I says, "Thrupley, be a man, and stow all this 'ere black'arted, bad temper;" I says, "come in and 'ave a cup of tea and a bit of supper with Brown and me, as only come 'ome late last night 'isself."

He says, "Go away, or I'll sprinkle you with this," a-threatenin' on me with the whitewash brush.

I says, "Oh! do be reasonable now as you're a grandfather, and as nice a little gal."

He stooped down at them words for to get a

fresh dip of whitewash, and I do believe meant to
give me a-duckin', but must 'ave over-reached 'isself, for he toppled over, steps, pail, whitewash, and
all; and there he was a-layin' in a reglar 'eap, as I
couldn't get at 'im thro' not bein' the figger for to
get thro' the top sash of a kitchen winder; but,
as luck would 'ave it, the lamplighter were jest
a-comin' by, as got in easy thro' the winder
and let me in, and we picked old Thrupley up
atween us, as were reglar stunned, but no bones
broke.

He were as wiolent as ever when he come
round, for the fust words as he utters were, " Turn
that old witch of Endor out;" leastways, it sounded
like witch, " or else I'll shy the pail at her."

So in course I weren't a-goin' to stay there to
'ave my back broke with a whitewash pail, so 'ome
I goes, and felt that chilly as I didn't think of nothing but our bit of supper and a mince pie as me
and Brown 'ad together, and went to bed with a
thankful 'art, a-thinkin' wot a mercy it were not
to be married to one of the elected, as is wot old
Thrupley calls 'isself; not as he'd ever be lected for
any place as I'd got a wote for, cos I don't consider
as he's fit for a beadle, nor a churchwarden, nor
nothink in the parochial line, as is lected about
Easter, with a nice row in the westry over it, as is
only a lot of jawin' 'umbugs, in my opinion; werry

nigh as bad as Parlymint, as is a reglar waste of time and money too.

It must 'ave been more than four years arter that time as I 'adn't never 'eard a word about that poor Emly Ryan, poor thing, as 'er 'usban' 'ad took 'er down in the country with 'im where he went a-actin', and I 'eard say was doin' werry nicely, and gettin' on to the top of the tree, as the sayin' is.

"Ah!" I says to Mrs. Flinders, the party as were a-tellin' me, "it's very easy to get to the top of the tree, but them as get there easiest sometimes 'as a bad fall, as in course is the wuss the 'igher as you falls from."

As to old Thrupley, he'd been moved away two years from our part, and went to live somewheres near 'is chapel, as they do say he is a-goin' to leave all 'is money to it; leastways, so Mrs. Flinders told me as it was jest on three years as I 'adn't set eyes on 'er, when she come in jest like old times, and we nat'rally got a-talkin' about old Thrupley, and then I says, "And what news of poor Emly?"

"Oh," says she, "why, she's a livin' over in the East End, as 'ad a engagement at one of them theayters."

I says, "To think as she shouldn't never have let me know."

"Oh," she says, "I thinks it's 'is doin', as ain't

come out the star as he espected, and I 'ave 'eard
say 'ave 'ad a bad illness, and there's four children,
and I don't believe it was over fifteen shillin's a-
week as he were earnin', as 'urt 'is pride."

"And enuf to 'urt anyone's pride too," I says;
" but what's 'er address ? "

She says, " Not far from Whitechapel Church."

" So," I says, " do get me the address, that's a
good soul; for go to see 'er I must."

It were two days arter as she come in agin, and
says, " It's close agin Lambeth Walk · as they re-
moved to, and Ryan is confined to 'is bed altogether
now, and 'ave been over three weeks."

I says, " Oh ! 'owever do they live ? "

She says, " Why, he gets 'elp from some of
them other play-actors, as is bad enuf off theirselves,
but always shares a crust with one another, leastways the parties as they live in the same 'ouse with
does by them, as is all theatrical; the father he's
utility, and the mother she did use to be a singin'
chamber-maid."

I says, " The utility line is wot we did all ought
to be to one another, but as to a singin' chamber-maid,
I wouldn't 'ave 'er in my 'ouse at a gift for I can't
a-bear a servant a-singin' about the place constant,
as is wot I wouldn't never allow."

" Oh ! " she says, a-smilin', " it's a line of busyness in a theayter."

"Oh!" I says, "indeed," cos in course I didn't know the purfessional ways, tho' she did, thro' 'avin' been a dresser, as 'ad retired along with the lady as she did used to dress, when she took 'er farewell, as they calls it, as allowed 'er a trifle to live upon, and with 'er own savin's she were pretty comfortable off, all but the roomatics, as was brought on by bein' all 'ours at the theayter, and often wet thro'

So I sent word to Mrs. Ryan thro' 'er, as I should like to come and see 'er, as sent me back word as she'd be glad to see me, tho' in great trouble; and off I went, with the weather that wet tho' not cold, as it werry often isn't at Christmas time, and found them Ryans in a second floor back, as was six in family thro' the last bein' twins under twelvemonth.

The eldest gal as I recollected being born she were a pretty child, and the second as brown as a gipsy, thro' bein' like 'is family, as inclined to the Mulatter.

They was all glad to see me, and, as to Ryan, I see wot were the matter with 'im in a instant, as were 'is liver and want of proper nourishment, as will pull a helefant down together, we all knows.

So arter we'd 'ad a bit of talk, I says, "I'm come to tea."

Says Mrs. Ryan, "I'm so glad," and I see 'er

give 'im a look, for he was a-settin' up by the fire, as give 'er a look back.

"But," I says, "I'm a-goin' to get somethink for your 'usban' "

"Oh!" he says, "I can't touch a bit."

"No," I says, " I know you can't, but," I says, "you must try and eat a bit of dry toast with your tea, and I'll get you somethink as'll do you good," and so I did, for I wouldn't let 'er slip out of the room, as were a-goin' to put away 'is boots under 'er shawl to get 'am and eggs and all manner for my tea if I 'adn't stopped 'er and got out myself and sent in the things as was wanted, and some medsin for 'im as I knowed would do 'im good, and lots of lemon-juice as he were to take every four 'ours, and took a turn from that very hour, and were better by Christmas-day, as I took 'em one of my puddin's over myself on Christmas-eve, not but wot it were more than 'is life were worth to touch a bit on it, but were pleased to see the children enjoy it, and 'ad some good strong beef-tea 'isself, and seemed to mend from the werry 'our as I fust see 'im.

They'd 'ad a orful time on it with bad busy-ness as they called it, as in my opinion all play-actin' is a bad busyness; but they must 'ave fine arts over it, for the way as them poor souls 'ad been supported by the others was wonderful, and now as Ryan were a-gettin' better, one of them tip-top actors sent 'im word as he'd better go out for a sea voyage as the doctors 'ad recommended, and if that there actor's good lady didn't come 'erself a-ridin' in 'er broom to see 'em, for I were there when she come, and if she didn't say as her 'usban would give 'im a 'undred pounds for to go over there as were Horsetralier, as he'd make 'is fortun at thro' bein' gold diggin's where they throwed the pure gold at the actors as they liked.

So I says to 'er, I says, " You'll escuse me, mum, but if your 'usban acts as well on the stage as he do off, why, he must be as fine a actor as the party I've 'eard my dear mother speak on as were only a boy; but all the world was a-breakin' of their backs for to try to get into the theayter and see 'im, as I think 'is name were Betty, not but wot that's more a gal's name than a boy's."

She gave a smile that lady and says, " Oh ! he was werry celebrated."

Them poor Ryans was pleased, and so was I for that matter, but I says to 'im, " You aint fit to travel yet, and 'ow will you manage to live till you starts ?"

Mrs. Ryan says as she didn't know.

I says, " Why not let your father know ?"

She says, " I did rite to 'im once, and only got a anser from a stranger as said he only rote as a minister of peace, but my father wouldn't never forgive me, and he could not in his dooty adwise 'im to."

"Oh!" I says, "this must be looked into. I'll go and see arter him;" and so I did that werry next day, as was a-livin' near the City Road Bridge.

It were a mean-lookin' 'ouse, and a gal opened the door, but a winegar-wisaged party come out of the parlour in 'er curl-papers when she 'eard me a-askin' for Mr. Thrupley, and says, "He don't see no one; he's in a 'appy state."

"Oh!" I says, "I'm glad to 'ear it. I'm an old friend, and should 'ave been glad to 'ave seen 'im."

All she says was, "You can't, and I wish you a good day."

I 'ad a friend, a old lady as lived close by there, as was Mrs. Pullman's 'arf sister, in the name of Kirby, so I went to see 'er as were pleased to see me, and took a friendly cup of tea and was a-tellin' 'er about me a-callin' at that 'ouse to see old Thrupley.

She says, "Oh!" she says, "a deakin at the chapel lives there, and I've 'eard say as there is a rich old loonytick as lives in the same house with them; and one gal as they had for a servant wouldn't stop cos they ill-treated 'im so, leastways that were whispered about."

"Ah!" I says, "parties will talk," cos I didn't

wish for to seem to 'ave no objic', so as she mightn't get lugged in no ways if there was a uproar. So I didn't stop long arter tea, and were a-goin' 'ome and 'ad to pass by that chapel where that minister preached, as Mrs. Kirby could see from 'er parlour-winder. The door were open, so I jest looked in and see as it were going to be service.

It were a cold, disertoot-looking place as all them chapels is, 'ad a acid smell about it, so arter looking round come out, and jest as I were walkin' away I see the minister a-goin' in with his good lady, and followin' them was that winegar-wisaged woman as a lanky feller with a taller face 'ad on 'is arm, as I knowed to be 'er as 'ad come to the door to me when I went to call on old Thrupley.

"Now," I says "is my time for to see 'im," so I goes back to the 'ouse, and knocks at the door. The same gal opened it as I'd see afore, so I says to her, "It's all right; I'm come to set with Mr. Thrupley a bit while the gentleman and 'is good lady is at chapel, and," I says, "I may want you to step as far as the doctor's for a little castor-ile." I says, "He's in the back fust floor, aint he?" as were only a guess on my part. "No," she says, "the back parlour, but," she says, "did Mrs. Grindley send you?"

I says, "Do you think as I should walk into a 'ouse if I didn't know wot I was a-doin' of," so I says, " show me a light, and I'll find a shillin' for you afore we parts."

The gal didn't seem 'arf to like it, but the mention of the shillin' seemed for to wake her up, so she showed me the light, and in I went, and in the back-parlour there was old Thrupley sure enough in a bed. Oh! such a mask of dirt and neglect.

So I says to the gal, "There's 'arf-a-crown, give me the light, and go at once and fetch the castor-oil, only mind you're in afore chapel is out."

" Oh!" she says, "that wont be till 'twixt nine and ten, for they've got a dippin' to-night, and sinners is a-goin' thro' the pool."

I says, " Then you needn't 'urry back, cos I shan't want the ile till the last thing."

I went up to the bed as soon as she were gone, and says, " Mr. Thrupley."

He says, " Oh," he says, "don't ask me, indeed I can't."

I see as he were between asleep and awake.

So I says, " You don't know me. I'm your old friend, Mrs. Brown, come to see you."

He says, " It ain't possible."

I says, " It is; and now tell me are you happy and comfortable 'ere?"

He says, a-sittin' up in bed, " Oh! take me away, that's a good soul; pray don't leave me 'ere, that orful woman."

I says, "Do they ill use you?"

He says, "Orful, and I do believe they'll murder me. I've lost the use of my limbs partial, and they won't let me send for a doctor."

I says, "Why didn't you send for your dorter?"

He says, "I did, I 'ave, but she sent me word as she wouldn't come."

I says, "Don't believe a word on it; they sent 'er word as you wouldn't see 'er, but," I says, "'ave you got any clothes?"

He says, "Yes, in that drawer."

So I goes to the drawer and rummages out 'is old clothes, as I helped 'im to put on, for he 'adn't quite lost the use of 'is limbs, but were werry 'elpless and rickety like.

I jest give 'is face and 'ands a bit of a rince, not in any 'urry, for it 'adn't struck eight by the time as he were dressed, as were a great fatigue to 'im, only I give 'im jest a drain out of my travelling flask as kept 'im up, and then I 'elped 'im to a chair and went to the door, and see a boy a-standin' there, and says to 'im, "Go and fetch me a cab, will you? and I'll give you tuppence."

He were off like a shot, and soon come back with one.

"Now," I says, "you're a good stout lad, lend me a 'and to 'elp a poor old gentleman into it; and it won't be no loss to you;" and so with 'is 'elp and

cabman's I got old Thrupley into the cab, and says
to the cabman, "You jest draw on to the corner and
I'll come in a minit."

I'd got a tin-box of old Thrupley's with me as
he'd give me, so I puts it into the cab and back into
the 'ouse I went and shet the door, and 'adn't been
in a minit when the gal come back with the castor-
ile as 'ad been 'avin' a nice jaw along with 'er pals,
no doubt.

So I says, " All right, you can keep the change,
and now I can't stop no longer to-night, and you
can give Mr. Thrupley the castor-ile if he asks for
it, and out of the 'ouse I whips sharp and into the
cab, and bowled off with old Thrupley as was
reglar done up, and got a wanderin' in his 'ead and
didn't know me, so there was nothink for it but to
take 'im to my place as were a-livin' in South
Lambeth then, and when I'd got 'im into the 'ouse I
sent the cab off for 'is dorter as come back at once,
and were overjoyed to see 'im tho' never a fond
father; as I sent for Mr. Brockley to see 'im that
same night, and said as he didn't think with all
our care as he could last many weeks at the most.

No more he didn't, tho' he got to be more 'isself,
and shook hands with Ryan as come to see him in a
cab, and made 'is will all over agin for he 'ad left
everything to that minister, and 'is deakin as they
called 'im, as come and ferreted 'im out a week

afore he died, and said as they was overjoyed for to know as he were friends with 'is dorter, and says the minister, " I will now go in and see 'im."

I says, " You're werry good, but he's a-dozin', and the doctor's orders is as he ain't on no account to be disturbed."

So I choked 'em off, and the next time they come the poor old man were quite insensible, and died like that in two days.

So Emly and her 'usban' agreed as that minister and 'is lot should be asked to the funeral, as they come to as black as crows, and when they come back from the symmetry, all come into my parlour and set down, and then that minister says to Ryan, " My good friend, you are no doubt aware as the worthy departed made 'is will in favour of those he loved," and out he pulls a paper as were old Thrupley's will, as left Emly fifty pounds.

Ryan was took aback, and as to Emly, she couldn't say nothing for surprise.

So the minister he went on to say, " We are willing to pay in reason for all the expenses of his illness and funeral, but can never forgive the way as he were carried off from the 'appy 'ome he 'ad with them as he considered 'is best friends as 'is will clearly shows."

I says, " 'Ow much has he left that good lady as took such care on 'im in that back-parlour ?"

Says the minister, "He 'ave left that worthy couple
a 'undred pounds apiece, and I'm residary legatee."

"Oh!" I says, "indeed."

"Yes," he says, "and here's the will all drawed up
proper and witnessed by strangers."

I says, "When did he make that will?"

"Oh!" he says, "it's more than eighteen months
ago."

"Ah!" then I says, "this as he made a month
ago will come fust," and I took out a paper and give
it to Ryan, as was old Thrupley's will made out by
a lawyer as 'ad known 'im for years and 'ad the
management of some 'ouses as he owned, as he'd
been and left, with some money in the Stocks, to
Emly and 'er children.

Says that minister, a-smilin', "And, pray, 'ow
much 'ave he left dear Mrs. Brown?"

I says, "Nothink, sir, for he paid me every ex-
pense, the same as he 'ad at the dirty dog-hole as I
took 'im out on."

That winegar-wisaged woman were a-goin' to
speak, but the minister he checked her, and says,
"No doubt Mr. Thrupley's dorter wont forget 'er
father's tried friends."

I says, "Tried is wot they did ought to be, and
conwicted to, but," I says, "we don't want no words,
so I wishes you a good day, and the sooner you're
gone the better I shall be pleased."

That minister said I were a worldling, but he loved me all the same; and they went off, that fieldmale a-sobbin', and the deakin a-opin' as I should be changed, and no doubt he wished as it might be into somethink unpleasant.

As to Emly and 'er 'usban' they was took by surprise, and so was I for that matter, cos I 'adn't no consumption, as that Old Thrupley were worth between three and four thousan' pounds, as were all tied up, but brought in nearly two 'underd a year.

But Ryan 'ad set 'is 'art on goin' that sea woyage, and it wasn't only 'is 'ealth as he were a-goin' for; but he said as he adn't never been precierated proper 'ere, and as he meant for to make 'em stare over there, and then come 'ome agin and play leadin' business.

So I says, "That's right; but," I says, "wotever you do, if you can't keep Christmas in winter, do jest 'ave a plum-puddin' one day that time of year for to remind you of 'ome, as I've give your wife the recipy on as they calls it; and then," I says, "preaps you'll remember me, as shall drink your better 'ealth on Christmas-day," for, tho' a deal more 'isself, yet was a-lookin' werry weedy and seedy, "and wish you many 'appy New Years, as I do all them as thinks with me about keepin' Christmas, as won't never go out of fashion not while one bit

of this world 'angs on to another; and if all the
Rooshuns as ever was born was to try and put it
down we should take and larf at 'em, and then if
they was sarcy over it take and punch their 'eads
agin like as we've done afore, not as we wants to
throw that in their faces; and shall 'ave to cover
up them monyments about the Crimeer when this
'ere young Duchess comes 'ome with 'er 'usban',
tho' she mayn't notice it thro' passin' quick in a
carridge and not a-readin' Inglish, and in course
he'll take werry good care not to pint 'em out
to 'er.

So I don't see arter all as we need care so
much, cos it ain't as if she was French; cos then
we must change Waterloo Place and Waterloo
Bridge, and 'ave the name took off the 'busses,
and make the Dook of Wellington call 'isself somethink else, so as not to 'urt 'er feelins.

But no doubt this 'ere young Duchess 'ave
plenty of sense in 'er 'ead, and won't go a-quarrelin'
over names; and I'm sure there ain't no nasty
feelin' over Roosher, nor nothink as comes from it,
for I'm sure them bears at the Jewlogical Gardens
is as much pampered as if they was Christshuns,
and as happy as the day's long, as the sayin' is,
a-playin' about in the water with a big lump of ice
for to suck and keep themselves cool; not as I
should care for to live in a tank like that, and be

always drippin' wet; but then, you see, I ain't a bear, nor yet a Rooshun neither, as must be wonderful people when you comes to think about Peter the Great, as were only a ship's carpenter— leastways worked like one, and then come to build that fine place as they calls Petersburg, I shouldn't care to live in with the ice a-breakin' up suddin arter a 'ard frost, when they can't 'ave 'ad a drop of water in them 'ouses for months, and froze too 'ard for to 'ave plugs in the street, and then to 'ave it come a-rushin' in with a suddin thaw to drown you, unless you gets out of the winder into a boat, when you 'ears a bell ring, as might be in the middle of the night or jest undressed, and give you your death, as you might as well be drownded as froze to death.

So I says, "Give me Old Ingland, as in course do 'ave 'ard frosts, but not out of all reason, tho' certingly the Tems 'ave been froze over twice in my mem'ry, but don't never last for more than six weeks, as is quite enuf, tho' better than six months.

But any 'ow we must 'ope for fine weather for to welcome 'er 'ome, poor thing, as will feel lone-some no doubt at fust among strangers, not but wot she'll find a mother twice over in Queen Wictorier, and that there sweet Princess of Wales for a sister, and in course will be a-goin' about a good deal; and then she'll settle down into a reg'lar Inglish wife, and I do 'ope won't go a-fidgettin' back'ards and for'ards to Roosher, as will only unsettle 'er, cos she did ought to know as when she's made 'er bed she must lay on it, as the sayin' is, whether it's Ingland or Roosher.

MRS. BROWN ON THE ROYAL RUSSIAN MARRIAGE.

I SAYS, "Marry a Rooshun? Never, Brown, it never wouldn't be allowed; as is werry near as bad as Catholics, I've 'eard say, besides a-bein' our nat'ral henemies, as we 'ad for to punch their 'eads over in the Crimeer."

"Yes," says Brown, "it's a rum match arter all the money and blood as we've wasted over 'em, as was that there Mr. Lewy Napoleon as let us into that 'ole."

I says, "And serve us right for follerin' sich a Jack-a-lantern, as the sayin' is; but," I says, "Rooshuns is better than Germins, as I can't abear that old beast of a Hemperor, nor yet that willin Beastmark. Besides, them Germins bein' sich a bullyin' lot, a-darin' for to dictate to us and a-ritin' to Queen Wictorier, a-sayin' as she wasn't to 'ave that feller Muller 'ung for murderin' old Briggs."

Not but Queen Wictorier 'ave give into them,

for I well remembers a Germin woman agin the City Road Bridge as cut 'er own child's 'ead off in the coal-'ole, as Queen Wictorier let off all thro' them Germins a-bullin' of 'er; and as to that Germin minister as were took up over a murder last Christmas, I do think as that did ought to 'ave been gone into more fully myself, so as to 'ave proved 'im innercent.

So I don't 'old with Germins myself bein' took for granted like that; tho' no doubt there's noble parties among them the same as Blucher, as the boots is called after. Why, he was a reg'lar hero, and they do say as 'ow if he'd been five minits later at the Battle of Waterloo the Dook of Wellin'ton would 'ave took and chucked up the sponge, as the sayin' is, as is a sign of wictory; so in course we knows as Germins is Germins, and not all like Muller and Beastmark, as thinks of nothink but robbin' and murderin' of their naybours, as'll come 'ome to 'em some fine day.

"Ah!" says Brown, "that's why it's a good thing for this 'ere Prince of ourn to go and marry one of those Rooshuns, as is strong enuf for to purtect 'is rights agin them Prooshuns."

I says, "I should like to see them Prooshuns dare for to interfere with 'is rights, as we should never stand them a-darin' for to interfere with any of Queen Wictorier's children."

Says Brown, " But this 'ere one he've got rights over in Germiny."

Then I says, " I'm sorry for 'im, for they don't know rights from 'rongs over there ; and poor Mrs. Sarmint as went over there along with 'er 'usban' to Berling about the railway, she said as they was all 'cathens as never went to church, but worked all day Sunday, and rediculed 'er for makin' 'er children say their prayers, and she'd 'eard one of their ministers say as the Bible were foolishness."

And I says, " They sings a werry different song when they comes 'ere to see Queen Wictorier, as'd pretty soon give 'em a good settin' down if they was to dare talk like that afore 'er, and that's the reason as she's a-goin' to send that there Dean Stanley over to marry them, cos in course he believes everythink, jest the same as the Archbishop of Canterbury, cos Queen Wictorier won't allow no larks over the Church, as she's the 'ead on."

" But," I says, " it's werry sing'ler ways for that there Dook of Edinburrer to like to go a-sailin' about in that there Black Sea, as must be like a-sailin' in a cesspool, as no doubt them Rooshuns is fond on thro' a-likin' lamp-ile, and 'orseflesh, and sour soup, tho' I 'ave 'eard say as they drinks delishus tea; but then you can't live upon tea."

And as to their a-sayin' as we can't never 'ave good tea thro' the sea-water a-spilin' on it, I bust out a-larfin' in Captin Malin's face, as were a-tellin' me about it, and says, " Why nobody never tried to make tea with sea-water, not even down at Margate, tho' in course there's no tellin' wot parties might 'ave done in a shipwreck."

He said it were the woyage as spilte the tea.

" Well," I says, " all as I can say we'd werry good tea a-goin' to Merryker, both out and 'ome."

" But," I says, " it'll be a good thing for that there young princess to get away from sich a place, for I've 'eard say as they never don't let their kings and queens die in their beds, but either strangles 'em or pisons 'em, the same as I've 'eard my dear mother say they did with the one as come over 'ere jest as I were born, with them other allied sufferins, as preaps is best put out of their misery, cos it must be werry dreadful for to be a crowned 'ead with murder always a-'angin' over it, jest like Mary Queen of Scots and 'er grandfather King Charles, as was murdered by that old warty-faced Crumble, as reg'lar upset the throne."

But then them Rooshun hemperors 'as the pull as long as it lasts, and ain't got no Gladstins, nor Brights, nor Odgers, to bully 'em, and ain't obligated to go and ask Parlymint for every farthin' as they wants, and can't 'ave their boots soled and 'eeled without gettin' the money from Parlymint, the same as that there feller as got up and made a row over the money for this 'ere Duke of Edinburrer, a-sayin' as the Queen did ought to support 'im and 'is wife and family, as is a likely story, poor dear soul, left a lone woman with nothink but wot Parlymint gives 'er, and if it was once known as she'd support 'er children, we should 'ave a nice starvin' lot come a-wantin' to marry into the family, and not nice, respectable parties, as can 'old their 'eads up with the best, the same as that young Lord as lives over in Scotland, as is a nice-lookin' young feller, as I see 'im a-dancin' that lively myself without no trousers, down in Scotland, tho' certingly 'is good lady were not a-lookin' on, as might not 'old with sich goin's on, though Queen Wictorier don't mind it a bit, and goes to see 'er servants all a-dancin' like that, as is their Scot free ways, and I 'ave 'eard say as all them young princes goes without 'em in Scotland, as makes clothes come cheaper no doubt; but must say as I 'opes as they don't take to 'em suddin, as must be a great change, unless somethink warm for underclothing, partikler a-walkin' up their mountins, as they goes up a-stalkin' arter them deers.

Not as it's a dress as would do for Roosher, I should say, where you gets froze to the coach-box in drivin' out, and comes 'ome frequent with your nose frozed off, as you're obligated for to take and berry it in the snow, or else would turn to mortification; so fancy wot it would be in a kilt—as don't reach your knees.

Tho' they do say that as that Hemperor of Roosher won't trust 'is dorter to us, not for all the year round, but will 'ave 'er 'ome for six months, as is all werry fine, but in course must depend on circumstances, as the sayin' is, and I'm sure she'll be took every care on 'ere in Ingland, with sich a royal ma-in-law as Queen Wictorier must be with all 'er esperience, and I'm sure as to nussin', they'd needn't be ankshus arter the way as we brought that there Prince of Wales thro' that illness as them 'ot sheep skins kep' alive, I'm sure we might be trusted with any Rooshun as ever were born.

Partickler arter the way as we took and nussed both sides over in the Crimeer, along with that good lady as must 'ave been the real two-'eaded Nightingale, to be clever enuf to manage all them wounded, along with a lot of ladies as went with 'er, as she kep' 'erself the 'ead on, tho' she were werry kind to 'em, and I 'ave 'eard say would send 'em nice things from 'er own table, cos in course thro' bein' 'ead, she 'ad to keep 'erself to 'erself, tho' the others was quite 'er equals, but in all them milingtary things, them as is in command must 'old up their 'eads.

Not as I thought much of that there lady's book wot she wrote about nussin', a-makin' out as there weren't no other disease but dirt, as is all my eye, cos we all knows as the cleanest may 'ave them disorders, as is wot flesh and blood is hair to, as the sayin' is.

But arter all said and done, that there fancy nussin' is all my eye, and if parties means to go in for it, they did ought to be reg'lar trained to it, and if they does it all free and for nothink, so much the better for 'em.

But no doubt that there Rooshun Princess won't find it cold enuf for 'er 'ere, as is used to everythink iced, like the polar bears at the Jew-logical Gardins, but then she can 'ave lumps of ice put in 'er bath for to play about in jest like 'im, as seem to enjoy it along with 'is ma, and stood a-watchin' 'em myself ever so long the last time as I were there, as proves as natur is natur, all over the world.

Not as I believe them Rooshuns come from bears, any more than that feller as wants to make out as we was all original monkeys, as certingly some boys is werry like I must say, and as to old Sinful, he were the baboon all over, as I'm sure must 'ave a tail, for of all the nasty, mischievous old warmin as ever I see he's the biggest, and the way as he tormented my cats proves it, an old beast; not as it were to pay 'im out as I drenched 'im with the syringe.

In course it's no use a-sayin' as you didn't go to do a thing if other parties says as you did it for the purpose, as I could take my oath were the last of my thoughts ever to do sich a thing over the wall.

Not as I can say as it were young Sam Belper's fault, as come in that same day as Brown sent in that syringe for to water the gardin with, as he took a pride in, and found the waterin'-pot that 'eavy as it tried 'is back, and more than I could lift if it were to save my life, and as to that gal a-doin' of it, why she'd take and drench the place like a pond, with 'er shoes and stockin's sopped thro' in no time.

So Brown he sent 'ome the syringe, with a lot of pipe to it, as he said I could 'ave the winders cleaned by it, and the outside of the 'ouse for that matter, from top to bottom.

So when young Belper saw it, " Oh ! " he says, " 'ow jolly, let's 'ave a try with it."

I says, " Do you understand its ways, cos I don't."

" Oh yes," he says, " it's as easy as pap. I'll show you."

So out he goes into the back garding, with me a-follerin' of 'im, an he puts one end of that there

pipe into the water-butt, and then begun a-workin'
away at the syringe as throwed the water down to
the middle border easy.

I says to 'im, " Sam, wotever you do, don't pint
it over the wall, cos," I says, "you may reg'lar
drown all Old Sinful's fowls, not as a little cold
water'd do 'im any 'arm, escept thro' never bein'
used to it, the shock might kill 'im."

Certingly it were werry useful in the way of
waterin' that syringe, and throwed the water agin
the back fust floor beautiful.

So Sam Belper he says, "The best way to
manage it is, for one to work at the pump and the
other to guide the syringe."

I says, " We'll try that way arter tea, as is jest
ready, so come in and 'ave some;" for I knowed as
all boys is always 'ungry, and a good tea he made,
with a good plate of cold rhubarb pie into the
bargin.

So when we had finished out we went agin, and
begun a-washin' down all the back washus door, me
a-'oldin' the syringe for to guide it, and Sam a-
workin' away at the other end.

I see as Old Sinful's back parlour winder were
open, and arter a bit he come a-climbin' out at it,
a-standin' on the winder-sill, a-nailin' of 'is creeper
round it, with 'is dorter a-'oldin' 'im by the legs.

Jest then Sam 'ad said to me, "Mrs. Brown,

haim at your staircase winder, as there's a lump
of mud on;" as I did accordin', but didn't
move it.

Says he, "Let's take off the nozzle, as will let
the water stronger."

So he come and unscrewed it for me, and out
flew the water in a reg'lar body, as the sayin' is, as
seemed quite to dazzle me; "But," I says, "I'll
'ave that bit of mud off, that I will, as I do believe
Old Sinful 'ad took and shied it out of spite."

I turned the syringe agin the winder, but some'ow
I got bothered, and Sam come and give my 'and a
twist for to guide the syringe, and the next thing
I 'eard were a scream and 'oller, and Old Sinful
gone.

I dropped the syringe like a red-'ot coal, and
runs up the back door steps to look over the wall,
and there he was a-layin' on 'is back all among 'is
tulips and daisies, as he'd jest planted.

I was thankful it were no wuss, and 'ollers out,
"I begs you ten thousand pardins, Mr. Sinful, as
were quite a accident."

Out come 'is dorter, as I could see were drenched,
and says, "You've killed 'im, as he's insensible."

I says, "Law, I 'opes not; I'll come in," for
we was friendly in those days, 'avin' made it up
over the cat, quite naybourly.

So in I goes, a-'urryin' thro' the 'ouse as soon

as the door were opened, and got into the garding,
and there was Old Sinful a-settin' on a bench a-
smilin', and only a little wet behind, thro' the water
'avin' gone between 'is legs, and caught his dorter
full in the face.

" So," he says, " that's a capital invention, Mrs.
Brown, I should like to see it closer."

" Oh! " I says, " that you shall with pleasure,"
pleased to think as he weren't offended; but it wasn't
no use a-askin' Sam Belper to give it me over the
wall, cos he'd been and cut away, and the gal was
in-doors, so I says, " I'll go in and 'and it you over
the wall, and you can use it in welcome; I am
thankful as there ain't no 'arm done, as we all
knows as a little cold water can't break no bones,
and 'your parlour winder ain't no great height to
fall from, tho' it might have shook you."

He didn't say nothink, only " Thank you, Mrs.
Brown, I should like to see that squirt."

So I goes in, screws the nozzle on, and 'ands it
to 'is dorter over the wall, and tells the gal to bring
me the steps, as I couldn't reach without.

She took it from me a-smilin', and gives it 'er
father, as asked me a many questions over it, as I
stood on the steps a-anserin', like the wolf and the
lamb for innercence, and didn't move not when he
put the pipe in the water, and throwed a lot all over
'is grass and gravel.

At last he says, "But this don't throw no large quantity of water."

I says, "No, you must unscrew the nozzle to get a lot out."

So he unscrews it, and 'is dorter she took and pumped away with it till it come out with great force, and then if that old wiper didn't take and play it like a fire plug slap in my face, as were jest my 'ead and shoulders over the wall, with the gal a-standin' at the foot of them steps to keep 'em steady.

If it 'ad been a cannon-ball sent slap at me it couldn't 'ave come not with no greater force, for it sent me a-flyin' back'ards, steps, gal, and all, as broke my fall, but pretty nigh stunned 'er; as to me, I was drenched to the skin, and were a-strugglin' 'ard to get on to my legs, and jest as I were on all fours, Old Sinful he come up the steps on 'is side, and pitches that syringe over the wall, as ketched me in the back, and sent me flat on my face, a-sayin', "Now, Mother Brown, you've 'ad a lesson 'ow to use a syringe another time."

I says, a-settin' up, "You've been my death and 'arf-stunned this poor gal."

"Ah!" he says, "I dare say you ain't more used to cold water than your naybours."

I'd 'arf a mind to 'ave shied a flower-pot at 'im, but that gal she were in sich a rage, that she

caught 'old of a clothes-prop, and give sich a drive
at 'im with it, that if he hadn't slipped down them
steps pretty quick she'd 'ave 'ad 'is 'ead 'arf off,
and would 'ave broke 'is winders if I 'adn't took
and stopped 'er, for she's Welsh, and when 'er
blood is up there ain't no keepin' 'er under.

So from that time there were a constant cool-
ness 'twixt me and Old Sinful, as were brought on
by that syringe, as he never will believe as I didn't
do for the purpose, and I must say as I 'as my
suspicions as Sam Belper 'ad a 'and in it, as, boy
like, is full of his tricks; but in course I didn't
want to get 'im blamed, partikler as Old Sinful 'ad
took the law in 'is own 'ands, as the sayin' is.

I must say as that gardin 'ave cost me a deal of
time and trouble, let alone the money, and I'm sure
I'd rather live in Roosher, where there aint no
gardins out-of-doors thro' it bein' all frost and
snow, and I'm sure I couldn't be always in a
'othouse as stifles me; and Brown he did take a
pride in his gardin, till he throwed it up along of
the cats as he wanted to shoot with a air-gun, as
in course I didn't mind, cos I knowed as air couldn't
kill nobody escept it were foul air, as in course
nobody wouldn't keep in a loaded gun, as might
explode like a coal-mine, as 'av'e been the grave of
many thro' lightin' of a pipe or forgettin' to take
their Davies afore goin' down into the pit.

But as to that gardin it's wuss than any coal-pit for bother, and I'm sure there's no tellin' when you are bein' robbed over it and when you ain't, and I'm sure nobody wouldn't 'ave looked for sich deception in a boy like that and a gardiner too, for he said he were only nineteen, and spoke kind of 'is aged grandmother bein' palsied, as throwed me off my guard a-thinkin' as she must be a weight on a young feller like that, as 'adn't no parents livin', leastways so he said, and were that thankful for the bit of bread and meat as I give 'im with 'arf a pint of beer, a-sayin' I were better than a mother to 'im, as he set and eat on the back-door step quite contented like.

Little did I dream when he asked me a-passin' by the gate with me a-standin' at the winder, if I wanted my garding done, as he were that mask of deception as he turned out.

For it did so 'appen as I did want the garding done, partikler the borders, as I've been a-turnin' over in my mind for more than a fortnight thro' the weather a-settin'-in fine, tho' two years ago now when I did use to take a pleasure in avin' that bit of garding tidy back and front, when Brown come 'ome, as tho' he didn't work in it now would like it to look neat.

In course it 'ad got to be a reg'lar wilderness with nothin' done for over a year, as the cats seemed for to glory in; not as our cat ever give 'em any encouragement, but would fly at 'em and send 'em a-rushin' over the wall like mad, and their skins a-flyin' in bits all about the place, if ever he caught 'em a-larkin' near our dust-'ole, as is a serous sort of a cat and that quiet in 'is ways as you'd think he'd knowed sorrers, and never so 'appy as when by the fireside, and always begin to purr as soon as ever the kittle begun to sing, as sounded werry cosy of a winter's evenin', and always looks like 'ome on the 'arthrug, leastways a footstool as I give 'im in front of the fire, thro' not a-likin' no low ways.

So as the days was a-gettin' out the year afore last, I says to myself as I'd 'ave the garding done back and front; tho' not a-meanin' to go a-spendin' money over the place as we was always a-talkin' of leavin', cos Brown says as I were a-fidgettin' to get into town.

"Well," I says to myself, "we shan't move this summer, and I shall spend five shillin's at the outside, besides the money I pays for the seeds and plants as I means to 'ave put in."

When I come to speak to Mr. Plumsole, as is a reglar gardener, about doin' what I wanted, he opened 'is mouth that wide, as the sayin' is, over the money, as made me draw in my 'orns.

So I says to him, "Bless you, I ain't a-goin' to

spend two pounds over it," as he said it would 'ave come to with new gravel and box, partikler as we weren't sure about stoppin'

So I let it go on till that young feller a-passin' and asking me the question, put it into my 'ead agin, as I thought would be a good opportunity, partikler as he said he'd do it all for 'arf-a-crown and turn the gravel, and come another day and bring some seeds and roots, as would only be a trifle.

He 'adn't got no tools with 'im, but a basket and a blue apon, as didn't matter, cos I'd got a spade and a rake, with a new birch-broom as I only bought the week afore.

So he set to work at once, and certingly he did make the front garding look werry tidy, as I were quite pleased with.

So when he'd had 'is bit of wittles, he says, "If it don't make no difference to you, mum, I'd rather begin the back garding with daylight to-morrer, as will make it lovely by tea-time."

"Well," I says, "I ain't no objection; not as I want's you 'ere by daylight a-ringin' me out of my bed; but seven is my time."

".Well," he says, "as you please."

"But," I says, "why not begin this afternoon, and take time by the firelock, as the sayin' is ?"

"Oh!" he says, "I've got a job next door jest

to do up the front, as I can manage this arternoon, tho' I must go 'ome for my tools to do it."

I says, "There's no occasion for that, cos," I says, "if it's only next door I'll lend you mine."

Cos it were not Old Sinful's side, but the other way, as is a widder lady as is serious, and goes of a Sunday to 'ear some one preach over the water, a-takin' of 'er lunch in her redicule, and 'as a cup of tea with one of the deakins, and don't get 'ome till close on ten at night, as is wot she calls a day of rest, but not to my notions, as likes a quiet life, partikler of a Sunday.

So that young feller were werry thankful, a-sayin' it would save 'im pretty nigh three mile of ground.

So he takes the spade and the rake and the broom, and I says, "You may have the syringe for waterin' if you likes."

He says, "Oh! thanks."

I says, "O! bother your 'thanks.' Why ever can't you say 'thank you, mum,' like a Christian, and not 'thanks,' as is wot them bus conductors and gals at the lunchin-bars bothers me with; and even the dustman come it with 'is 'thanks' when I give 'im tuppence for takin' away my dust-'ole."

Well, that chap 'ad got 'is 'ands pretty full with the other things, so I says, "You may as well leave the syringe, and come round for it if you wants it."

He says, "Oh! I can manage it under my arm."

I says, "No, you can't, as'll go a-droppin' of it and bend the nozzle," so I takes it away, and off he goes.

Next door the other way 'ave got the entrance round the corner, and, tho' I can see the back gardin from my back parlour winder, I can't see the front escept from my bed-room, as I didn't go up to thro' 'avin' of my 'ands full a-darnin' of my best tablecloth, as I set a-doin' in the back parlour, as I'm sure Mrs. Giddins must 'ave washed with some of them bleachin' liquids, as may be all werry fine for Queen Wictorier to use in 'er own laundry, as they say she do, and saves them maids-of-'oner a deal of trouble, as in course don't care about a-standin' at the royal wash-tub longer than they can 'elp; but all them things, in my opinion, makes your linen drop into 'oles.

I kep' on a workin' till I 'eard it go five, as is my tea-time when not espectin' Brown by the tram, as in course I waits for if it's 'arf a 'our or so, and up I gets and goes to the top of the stairs, and says, "'Liza Ann, why don't you bring up the tea-things?"

She says, "I'm a-waitin' for the milk."

I says, "If your kittle's on the bile you can bring up the things, and by that time the milk is sure to be round, or else you can run for it, as is only jest round the corner."

Well, she brought up the things, and took away the tea-pot, thro' bein' a gal as I can trust not to make it till the steam's a-comin' out at the spout; but no milkman never come round, as I could see were a-makin' the cat werry anxious in 'is mind.

So the gal she run for it, but met the man at the corner with it 'as 'ad one of 'is pails kicked over by a pony-cart in the Bow Road.

So the man he stopped to scrve 'er at the corner, and when she come in she says, " Didn't that gardener say he were a-goin' to work at Mrs. Calton's front garding?"

I says, "In course he did, and not afore it wants it."

" Well," she says, " he ain't there nor yet been there, for it's jest as it 'ave been ever since I come 'ere, as is over six weeks now."

I says, "He's thought better on it; but," I says, " aint he brought back them spades and things ? "

She says, " No, he ain't been near the place."

Well, a-knowin' as the tea, if left,would be drored to death, and not a-carin' about Mrs. Calton, I sent the gal to ask if the young man were there, as come back and said as Mrs. Calton 'adn't never set eyes on him or yet spoke to 'im.

So then I see, in course, as he'd been and lewanted with my property, as is a-warnin' to me never to employ them permiscous fellers at the gate, as is as bad as the flyin' dustmen did used to be.

Not as I give up all 'opes till the week were out, a-thinkin' as he might come back, and a-feelin' thankful as he 'adn't took the syringe as well, as is enuf to make you set your face agin doin' any one a good turn, tho' they may 'ave a bedridden grand-mother on their 'ands.

But, as I were a-sayin', I can't think 'owever we shall get on with that young Princess as is a widder, I suppose, cos 'ow else can she be a Grand Duchess, as in course must 'ave 'ad a Grand Duke for a 'usban', as is why Queen Wictorier let 'er dorter marry that young Scotchman, cos them Scotch Dukes is always orful grand, tho' they walks about like the rest without, as I considers, proper clothes to their backs, for it give me sich a turn when I were in Scotland as a young Scotch laird, as they calls 'em, as means lord, he come up and spoke to me in the pourin' rein, with a long white Mackintosh on, as is a Scotch inwention agin the rain, with 'is umbreller up.

He were werry perlite, a-sayin' as he were werry glad to see me in Scotland agin, as we went to last year as far as 'Obun, where I've been afore.

He were that perlite a-walkin' with me to where
I were a-goin' to lodge, a 'oldin' of 'is umbreller
over me, and me a-thinkin' as he were dressed
proper under that Mackintosh, and you might 'ave
knocked me down with a feather when we got to
the door, £ nd he took off 'is Mackintosh for to give
it a shake, and 'adn't got on no unmentionables, as
the sayin' is.

I says, " Mussy on us, you'll ketch your death
in sich weather as this, as might as well come out
in your night-gownd, with a drizzlin' rain and a
'igh wind a-blowin' you about, but he didn't mind
it a bit, and then," as I says, " to go like that to a
dance, as in general is a place as parties dresses
theirselves to go to, but the Scotch reg'lar un-
dresses and dances about as free as the hair, as the
sayin' is."

I certingly did see Prince Leopold dressed like
that 'imself, as in course only did it thro' bein' on a
wisit to one of them Scotch dooks; and wouldn't
'ave done it if 'is Royal Ma 'ad known, cos he's far
from strong I've 'eard say, tho' no doubt flannin
next the skin; but I do 'ope if they goes to Roosher
to see their Royal brother married, Queen Wictorier
will make 'em promise not to dress Scotch-like, or
they'll be froze up, and did ought to 'ave fleecy
'osery under-clothing, for I'm told it's wuss than
Canader, as I've been to, where you can't walk out

without a icicle at the end of your nose, and your
ears bunged up with wool.

I certingly should like to see them weddin' dresses
of that there Grand Duchess, and do 'ope as that
there Rooshun pa of 'ern will come down 'andsome,
and not be espectin' us to find her treuso, as we've
'ad to do afore now, and I'm sure as Queen Wictorier
would be put to 'er wit's end, as the sayin' is, to
get the things made now, if it's to come off in
Janivary, for wot with the 'igh price of coals and
the work as young women can get at the Telegraph,
you can't get no work done 'ardly for love or money,
as the sayin' is, and that's why if I were Queen
Wictorier I certingly should buy them made-up
costumes, as is werry becomin', and a savin' in the
end ; and in course them Rooshuns as is used to go
about in their bare skins don't mind 'ow things is
made, and as to that I'm sure you can't get nothink
made decent, and if Queen Wictorier were to ask me
I'm sure I couldn't recommend 'er a dressmaker
arter the way that last one served me, as I should
call a reg'lar thief, and as to Mrs. Blocket a-sayin'
as she were a fust-rate dress-maker, thro' bein'
French, it's all rubbish, cos tho', in course, every
one knows as there ain't nothink like the French to
dress when they are dressed, as I'm sure some on
'em wants it, as I've see as plain women as ever
stepped over in Paris, and, as to dress, some of 'em

sweepin' the streets without 'ardly a rag to their backs.

So all the French is not always well dressed any more than their betters.

"But," I says to Mrs. Blocket, " I shouldn't like to 'ave it spilte, as will require to fit like wax, as the sayin' is, or won't look well thro' being dyed, and a satin Turk; as I've 'ad by me for years, and were a brown, but 'ave took a rich maroon, as is a dressy colour for my time of life, and will look grand with my hamber shawl and green ribbins in my bonnet, as is black lace, with a poppy.

When this ere French woman come in I didn't some'ow fancy 'er, tho' reg'lar French, with a mow-'air front, and a black silk back to 'er cap as I never do fancy myself.

She took snuff and wore glasses, as made 'er eyes 'ave a reg'lar glare in 'em; when you looked at 'er straight in the face.

I some'ow 'ad my misgivin's when I set 'er to work at our back parler winder, and brought 'er down the stuff, with a sarcer of pins, for she says, " Ah, never, I shan't 'im fit to your shape, as is that big fat."

I says, " Madam, you've come 'ere to work, and not for to make remarks on my figger, as did not make myself."

" But," she says, " never is there the stuff

for you, as would not be enuf to make 'em for a chile."

I says, "Go along with your nonsense; why it were sixteen yards, as is ample, and silks don't srink in dyin' is well beknown."

So, I see as she'd make a mull on it, and thinks I to myself, I won't 'ave it cut to waste, and preaps 'ad better give 'er my poil de chev, as they call it at the shop, to make up.

So I brought it 'er down, and showed 'er in a fashion book as she brought along with 'er, 'ow I should like it made with flouncies round the skirt.

I'd promised jest to give a look in at Mrs. Belper's oppersite, thro' 'er not a-doin' as well as I could 'ave liked to see 'er with twins, and never easy in my mind till three days is over, so 'avin' give that French catamarang the stuff, away I goes so as to be 'ome in time to give 'er a bit of dinner, as is a thing as them as goes out to work don't get every day comfortable ; so says to the gal, " Mind, if I ain't in, let madam 'ave 'er bit of 'arrico nice and 'ot, at one o'clock, with a pint of ale, as she she'd said she'd like."

I'd made that 'arrico with my own 'ands, and a bread-and-butter puddin'

I found Mrs. Belper wery low, and a nuss as were serious a-sheddin' tears over the twins, a-sayin' as it would be a blessin' if they was took too.

I says, "Go along with your rubbish; both mother and children is a-doin' well, but," I says, "you musn't let her get too low."

I see it wasn't no use a-talkin' to that woman, as 'ad a tear a-standin' constant in 'er eye.

So I sent one of the boys off for 'is grandmother and stopped along with Mrs. Belper till she come, for the poor soul told me as that nuss were a reglar ranter, and 'ad stood at the bottom of that poor creetur's bed a-givin' of 'er speritial comfort for over a 'our the night afore, as were Sunday.

I didn't get back 'ome till jest on three, and when I got into the back parlour there set Madam a-doin' some braidin'

She says, "Ah! Missis Brown, I tort that there never should be enuf stoff."

I says, "Wot do you mean? Why, there's seventeen yards ; wot 'ave you done with it?"

"Oh!" she says, "when I cut de flounce there was only enuf left for de body and sleeve."

I says, "Mussy on us woman, why, wotever 'ave you been about?" for I looked the other side of 'er chair and see all my stuff in a 'eap on the ground cut into flouncins.

She says, "Oh! yes, 'ere is de flounce, but now I want the skirts to put 'im on."

I thought I should 'ave dropped, for there if she 'adn't been and cut up all the stuff for flounces.

I felt as if I could 'ave give 'er the umbreller over 'er 'ead, but knowin' as that wouldn't be the lady to a forriner, I says, " Madam, bong jaw, there's my door."

She says, " Ah! you do not wish me to stop to-day; I will come to-morrow then."

I says, " No you won't, nor never no more."

" Ah! then," she say, " you pay me seven shillin' sixpence."

I says, " Wot for ? "

She says, " Three day, 'arf-a-crown a-day."

I says, " Wot 'ave you got in your foolish 'ead ?"

She says, " Mrs. Blocket tell me you shall want me three days the very least."

I says, " Rubbish, I never said so, and wot's more, I didn't ought to pay you at all arter spilin' my stuff, as is only eighteen pence a-day."

She jumps up, puts all 'er things in a good-sized black bag, and a-clawin' on 'er bonnet and jacket, says, " Ah, ah! I am sorry I ever come to you as cannot work for the pigs."

I says, " Come, none of your impidence; walk out with you, do," and I opens the door.

I says, " I shall tell Mrs. Blocket of your impidence, and if she says you're to be paid, I'll give 'er the money."

She says, " You a nasty fat old thing, ah !" and she put out 'er tongue at me.

I never did feel more inclined in my life to give any one a leg down my front steps, but wouldn't forget myself, and out my lady marched.

I says, "Hi, stop here ! you've been and left your old sack behind you," as she'd put down in the passage while a-fastenin' of 'er jacket." I takes it up and shies it arter 'er down the steps, a-sayin', "Never dare come near me agin, or I'll give you in charge."

I could 'ave cried with wexation when I went back into that room, and see all my beautiful stuff a-layin' in a 'eap, cut to ribbins, as the sayin' is ; and says to myself, "It's a mussy as I didn't trust the sating Turk to her, but," I says, a-lookin' round, "wherever 'ave she put it," for I couldn't see it nowhere about.

So I calls to the gal and says, "Where did that French fish-fag put my bit of silk ? "

She come a-runnin' up, and says, "I've never see it since I come to tell 'er as dinner were ready, and it were a-layin' on this chair.";

"Yes," I says, "that's where I put it when I brought her down the 'poil de chev' to make instead on it; why surely she can't never 'ave took it away with 'er in that black bag ? If so, she's a reg'lar thief."

So as I'd 'ad a snack at Mrs. Belper's and 'ad my bonnet on, I thought as I'd go at once to Mrs. Blocket, so did accordin'.

She was jest a-goin' to tea when I got there, and when she'd 'eard all as I 'ad to say,

She says, "Well, of all the deep artful desinin' wretches it's that woman as 'ave been 'ere, a-sayin' as you'd been and treated 'er shameful, and give 'er a meal as were enough to make a dog sick, and then wouldn't pay her, but got 'er to take some old bits of dyed rubbish of silk as she showed me, instead of her money."

I says, "Old dyed rubbish indeed, why, it's my sating Turk, as 'ave dyed equal to new. I'll 'ave the perlice arter 'er."

"Well," says Mrs. Blocket, "'ow will you prove as you didn't give it 'er, as you owns to not 'avin' paid 'er?"

I says, "Do step back with me and see the 'avoc she 'ave made of my 'poil de chev.'"

"Why," she says, "she told me as you said you wanted plenty of flounce all round and round you, as would cut into stuff, and then when she 'ad cut em off you took and turned 'er out of the 'ouse."

"Well," I says, "if she'll say that she'll say anythink, but," I says, "I'll summons her for my satting Turk, and 'ave it too as sure as eggs is eggs, as the sayin' is."

I couldn't sleep for thinkin' of that woman being such a wile falsehood, and wowed as I'd 'ave the law on 'er by mornin's light, tho' Brown he did say,

" Let 'er alone, cos, " he says " it's only wastin' time and money to try and get the law of them thieves, so," he says, " if you takes my adwice you'll leave it alone, for I never knowed any one as got their rights by goin' to law, as is made to protect the thieves, I do believe."

"Well," I says, " I'll go to the perlice about it, as may frighten 'er into givin' of it up," and off I was, tho' as I got near the place my 'art misgive me, for I can't abear the sight of them law places, tho' no doubt they means to do right by you.

I says to the gentleman as I see at the Perlice Court, as was wonderful perlite, " I'm come for to take out a summons for my satting Turk as she've been and carried off, tho' she may say as I give it 'er, thro' certingly 'avin' shied the bag arter 'er down the steps, but hadn't no consumption as my dress were in it."

Says the party at a desk, " Pray calm yourself, my good lady, and do speak plainly ; wot is it you want ?"

" Why," I says, " a summons."

" Against whom ?" he says.

" Why," I says, " 'er name is Seversack, I be-lieve, tho' don't know 'er Christian name, nor yet 'er address, but did live close agin Mr. Marble, the butcher, as is near Wellclose Square."

" ' 'Ow," he says werry kind, " my good soul, 'ow

5

can I give you a summons when you don't know wot it is you wants yourself?"

I says, "Oh! yes I do, and will speak to the magistrate myself, as is my rights."

"Oh!" he says, "very well, with all my 'art."

So I leaves 'is room, and goes in at the door of the Perlice Office where all parties enters as wants to 'ear wot's goin' on, and a nice lot there was as was a-goin' on about a willin as 'ad been and broke 'is wife's ribs thro' jumpin' on 'er, as stood there a-cryin', and wanted to get 'im off.

That magistrate he wouldn't stand none of that gammon, but give 'im three months on the spot, as served 'im right in my opinion.

Well, arter that he were jest a-gettin' up that magistrate were, and a-goin' out of the place, when I says, "Escuse me, my Lord, as it's your worship I would say, but can't I have a summons agin that French fieldmale as 'ave got my property?"

Says the magistrate a-turnin' back, "Wot is she talkin' about?"

"Why," I says, "I'm a-talkin' about a satting Turk as that Frenchwoman took away in her sack, as she called it, as I throwed arter 'er, unawares as she'd got it."

He says, "Wot is it you're a-sayin' about a Turk as a Frenchwoman put in a sack? Is it a case of murder like Waterloo Bridge?"

"Oh, no," I says, "I don't think as she'd commit a murder, but she'd swear away any one's life, and wot I wants is justice, as I didn't ought to be kep from jest because I don't appear to know 'er Christian name, as may be a Jew for all I knows, as never don't have none, tho' they calls theirselves Jacobs and Josephs, as is Christian names all the world over."

Says the magistrate, "Clerk, pray attend to this person, as seems confused in 'er 'ead."

"Yes," I says, "and well I may be a-settin' up as I 'ave been two nights this week with a friend with twins as is barely out of danger now, and am afraid may fly to 'er 'ead, tho' it is almost a week, leastways five days."

Says that party as I'd spoke to first a-comin' in, "Really your worship, I can't make out wot the good lady wants."

I says, "Cos you won't listen to what I'm a-sayin', as is as plain as the nose on your face, as the sayin' is; as is my property took away surreptitious, as never wont 'ave nothink more to do with no forriners; and wouldn't this time but for Mrs. Blocket a-recommendin' of 'er like a sister."

So that magistrate he says, "Attend to 'er, will you, and see wot she wants," and out he walks, as is not wot I calls doin' justice: but. law, I dessay he were goin' arter 'is lunch, as is the way of the world, every one for theirselves, partikler at meal-times, as we all requires.

When I come to talk to that clerk, I do believe as he were a downright loonatic; for if he didn't go on about sich a lot of rubbish as made me get that wild as I walks out of the place, and goes back to Mrs. Blocket for to get more information about that French 'ussey, and, when I got there, who should I see a-settin' there but the werry party 'erself.

I didn't take no notice, but waited for 'er to speak, as Mrs. Blocket interrupted 'er a-doin' a-sayin', "Oh! Mrs. Brown, it's all right; Madam 'ave brought back your silk as she 'adn't no idea she'd got in 'er bag, as she says you must 'ave put it in yourself, and certingly it aint much to make a row over."

"No!" says that old French cat; "never I see 'im till last night, when I open my sack, and then I say, 'Wot rubbish 'ave I got 'ere?'"

I says, "Wot are you a-callin' rubbish?"

"Well," says Mrs. Blocket a-chimin' in, "I must say it aint much account;" and she brings for'ard a dirty-lookin' bit of paper as the pieces of my satting Turk fell out on.

You never in your life see such crumpled-up, greasy, spotty bits of stuff in your life.

I says, "That old beast 'ave been and wrapped it up in a dirty bit of paper for the purpose of s'ilin' it, and, in my opinion, 'ave put it in that bag with 'er filthy comb and brush; not as she ever washes either."

"Oh!" says the Frenchwoman, with a scream, "you call me old cat, you old pig; and I will scratch your 'ead and blow your nose for you."

I says, "You dare lay one of your dirty French fingers on me, and I'll lock you up."

Says Mrs. Blocket, a-interferin', "Oh! Mrs. Brown, remember as she's a forriner, and I can't see 'er put upon."

I says, "Who wants to put on 'er? And as to bein' a forriner, she's none the better for that, as we all knows may be a reg'lar Deeblang, as murdered the old woman in Park Lane, and did ought to 'ave been 'ung."

"Oh!" says Mrs. Blocket, "don't insult 'er over that, as 'adn't no 'and in it."

I says, "I don't know that."

Says that old Frenchwoman, "Wot that you say, as I'm a murderer? Ah! I shall make you prove 'im. You would ruin me of my character, would you? Ah! ah! we will see! we will see! And you, Madame Blocket, are a witness, and to prison you shall go." And out of the place she bounces.

Says Mrs. Blocket, when she were gone, "Oh! Mrs. Brown, 'ow could you illude to that murder, as, in course, goes 'ome to all forriners? and, in course, it were only a forriner as she murdered; and if they likes to do it to one another, in course it aint no busyness of ourn."

"Well," I says, "Mrs. Blocket, them aint my views, as wouldn't set by quiet and see the biggest forriner as ever were born murdered before my eyes in cold blood. But," I says, "that's a wile old 'ag, for did you ever see anything in sich a mess as this 'ere satting, as come from the dyer's like new?"

"Well," says Mrs. Blocket, "there never wouldn't 'ave been enuf to make you a dress, for there's only five breadths and a 'arf."

I says, "There were seven come 'ome the same as seven were sent, and the two backs and sleeves, and plenty for the rest of the body; but now it's all creased and greased so, I never couldn't 'ave it made up if it were all here; as in course that old fish-fag 'ave purloined the best bits."

Says Mrs. Blocket, "I think you're 'ard on er."

I says, "I don't think as you did ought to 'ave recommended 'er to me, as is no more a dressmaker than I'm a drummer-boy."

"Well," she says, "I'm sure she'd 'ave been wuss than a reg'lar thief if she'd made up this dyed rubbish for you, as wouldn't 'ave come down to your knees, nor yet 'ave met 'arf round you; and a nice figger you'd 'ave looked." And if she didn't take and bust out a-larfin.

I says, " I dessay it's werry amusin', and I'm sure any one could tell as she made your things, as don't fit you any more than a 'op-sack. But," I says, " I won't give you any more of my company, and can do without yours."

So I took up my bits of my dress as that old thief had left, and out of the place I walked, and aint seen Mrs. Blocket since; and met that French creetur three months arter in the Mile End Road, with a bonnet on and a jacket to match, as I could swear was both made out of my satting Turk as sure as London is built of bricks and stones.

So no more French dressmakers for me, cos, tho' they may 'ave werry good taste—as that old thief proved in usin' of my satting Turk—yet it's 'ard to 'ave your things stole, and to see 'em a-lookin' that becomin' on another's back as 'ave no right to be a-wearin' on 'em, but I ain't no biggert for all that.

And I don't know as I ever should 'ave give this 'ere Rooshun marridge a thought over the religion, if it 'adn't been thro' Mrs. Tremlitt, as takes them things to 'art, and says as the Jeserists is a under-mindin' our Constitution, and as this 'ere Rooshun religion is nearly as bad, thro' a-woshupin' picters,

tho' not a-believin' in gravin imiges, and will 'ave
it as saints is saints, the same as the Catholics.

Mrs. Trimlett, she's one of them as is reg'lar
at 'er chapel twice of a Sunday, and two evenin's
a-week besides, as in course is quite right in 'er,
a-considerin' of it a dooty, as she do, as I'm werry
glad I must say as I don't, for of all the little dirty
dismil 'oles as ever I put my nose in, as the sayin'
is, it's the closest, and I'm sure them as goes there
didn't ought to 'ave no noses, and I don't believe
as they can 'ave none, for I'm sure I wish I could
'ave left mine at 'ome, for I reg'lar 'eaved agin,
with every winder shet for fear as the minister
should take cold, as blowed 'is nose a reg'lar blast,
and 'owled over the woes as was a-comin' on us till
he nearly give me the jumps, and made lots on 'em
weep.

I thought as Mrs. Trimlett would 'ave choked,
thro' bein' that lusty as 'er sobs can't get a proper
went, as is the way with them as 'ave got fat about
the 'art, and I'm sure she must 'ave got it about 'er
everywhere, as 'arf 'er time is took up a-lettin'
things out, as she will 'ave made too tight at fust,
and quite lost 'er temper over bein' told in goin' to
buy a costoom as she were nearly two yards round
the waist, leastways that's the stuff as it took to
make 'er a dress, for there wasn't a costoom to fit
'er, and not set in gethers neither.

I didn't think as she'd ever come out of Bethesder alive that time, as I went with 'er, and don't
believe as she ever would, if somethink 'adn't give
way in 'er waistband, as seemed for to relieve 'er, as
I told 'er was foolishness to try and force natur like
that, and when that minister kep' a-goin' on about
bein' girded up, I thought to myself as it were
thro' a-follerin' of 'is adwice that she 'ad laced
'erself that tight as werry nigh 'ad a fit, and would,
too, in the werry pew, if I 'adn't 'ad the presence
of mind to cut a string for 'er with my silver fruit-
knife, as I always carries in my pocket, as the point
on is worn that sharp that I do believe you could
bleed anyone with it at a pinch, as the sayin' is.

So when we come out of that chapel I says,
" Mark my words, Mrs. Trimlett, if you perseweres
in bein' drawed in that tight, you'll end in a fit."

" Oh !" she says, " you're quite mistook ; my
things was a-comin' off thro' easiness, but it was 'is
piercin' words as seems to go thro' your marrer
like."

Well," I says, " I don't know anything about
your marrer ; all I can say is, that you went off like
a gun when I cut that broad tape as goes round
you."

Well, jest then she give a stumble like, as was
thro' 'er skirtin' a-fallin' round 'er feet; and I
didn't know what would come next, so 'ailed a cab

as were a-passin', and 'ome I took 'er, and only jest
in time, for I'd been and cut away her mainstays, as
the sayin' is, and she'd 'ave been a mask of ruins
all over the pavement if any one 'ad run agin er, or
brushed by 'er.

She were dreadful put out with wot she called
my interferin' ways, a-sayin' as it weren't nothink
to do with tight-lacin' 'er bein' took bad, but only
'er groanin' in sperrits.

" Well," I says, " I wouldn't stand by and 'ear
anyone say it of you;" for she'd been a-spendin' the
arternoon with me, and beyond a mere smell as she
took in 'er tea, as weren't 'arf a glass, I'm sure no
sperrits 'adn't crossed her lips, for I ain't one to incourage no one in tipplin', as I'd been told she did
on the quiet, tho' I always says as it's a fine medsin
if took in moderation, and have known it to save
life, as 'll be my solim words to my dyin' day, and so
I'd tell the Archbishop of Canterbury 'imself, as
'ave turned tea-totaller, they do say, thro 'avin' got
a interest in them Lambeth waterworks, as is jest
the same as other bishops as I've 'eard on, as one on
'em 'ad a deal of property thro' 'is wife in the distil-
lin' line, so in course wouldn't be no teatotaller."

And as I says, a-sayin,' " Why should he be, as
there aint no more sin in drinkin' than in eatin',
if took in moderation, as is my maxim thro' life."

But as I says to Mrs. Trimlett, I says, " Wot ever

'ave we got to do with 'er religion if she is a
Rooshun, as don't care wot she believes, the same
as Queen Wictorier, jest believes wot she likes,
as when she's in Scotland goes to them kirks, as is
dreadful dull work for them young people, I should
say, as don't 'ave no picters, nor yet even a orgin,
as do wake you up arter a long sermin, as is wot
the Scotch likes, and wont 'ave a orgin to wake 'em
up, as they considers a idol."

So I says, " Let this 'ere Rooshun lady 'ave 'er
own ways, and let 'im 'ave 'is'n ; and as to ̱the
children, in course they'll be brought up like the
School Board, with no religion at all, as is the law
of the land nowadays, and in course the Royal
Family did ought to set a good esample, and keep
to the laws, and won't learn no Catechism, nor nothink like that."

But as to edicatin' children not to believe in
nothink, that's not my ways, tho' I'm sure my life's
a reg'lar burdin to me, as the sayin' is, and all thro'
this 'ere edication, as is what I calls a reg'lar in-
quisition a-comin' into your 'ouse, and a-askin' if
you've got any young children, as is a question as
put poor Miss Lunn that out when the party asked
it 'er at 'er own door, as she walked straight
into 'er front parlour and 'ad a fit of 'sterrics, afore
she could get to 'er sofy, and dropped into the
fust chair as she come to like a stone, as is a 'eavy

weight, poor thing, and shouldn't 'ave credited it if I 'adn't been a-settin' there 'avin' of a chat with 'er, when the knock come to the door, as she run out to anser, and then to 'ave such a question put to 'er, plump afore the pot boy, too, as 'ad come up to the door, with the 'leven o'clock beer, for the woman as 'ad been at the wash-tub since seven constant, so required 'er half pint; and certingly never see a finer infant, under the month, as the little gal 'ad jest brought, as shows that 'ard work don't make no difference.

I'd jest dropped in myself to see Miss Lunn over my corsets, thro' 'er bein' in that line, and 'er mother before 'er, as don't do much at the business now, but were a-givin' a eye to the 'angin' out, from the back parlour winder, as can't get out of 'er chair thro' weak jints, and a-shellin' a few peas, as they was a-goin' to 'ave with a bit of gammon of bacon, and the best end of the scrag of mutton for downstairs, as they sent to the oven, with some taters under it, and a bit of batter; as in course it wouldn't be fair to espect a woman for to wash all day on bacon and peas, partikler the fust time as she'd been out, as were under three weeks, as she did so as not to disappint Mrs. Lunn, as 'ave knowed 'er from a gal, tho' she 'ave got a steady 'usband in the plasterin' line, but wotever is eighteen shillin' a week to marry on, partikler with things such a price, partikler butcher's meat, as is a-runnin' quick on to famine.

But, as I were a-sayin', I'd brought Miss Lunn my last pair, thro' the shoulder-strap a-wantin' easin', for I always sticks to my old ways, I don't care about being moulded by steam, nor nothink, as may look a lovely figger, but couldn't bear to be squeezed like that agin a wall myself, any more than them French inventions, as is like a clamp to fasten in front, as werry nigh suffercated me that time as I tried them on, and couldn't get 'em undone, and thought as I never should 'ave drawed a straight breath agin from my 'art, and if Brown 'adn't come in, as run down agin quick for the carvin' knife, and took and ripped me up the back, there'd 'ave been a end of me.

" So," as I says to Mrs. Lunn, " I shall stick to my laces to the end, as is quite figger enuf for me."

Miss Lunn, she'd jest seen where they wanted lettin' out, when the tap come as she went to anser, little dreamin' as she were a-goin' to 'ave 'er character took away like that, as may be the edication boards' ways, but not manners, to ask a single party about 'er 'avin' young children, and then foller 'er into the parlor, as were a-sobbin' like any infant in arms, on that black 'orse 'air sofy, as made me say to 'im, " Wotever is the reason? " a-thinkin' nat'rally as pre'aps she were behind with the water rate, and as he were the collector, a-puttin' on the screw, a-presumin' on it bein' washin' day; but when he began a-talkin' about edication, then I see where we was, and knowed as he were comin' a-spyin' for to get parties fined as didn't send their children to school.

I must say as I were put out, and says to 'im, " Pray, wotever busyness is it of yourn whether this lady 'ave got young children or not, as is 'er busyness ? "

Miss Lunn give another shriek and says, " Oh ! Mrs. Brown, pray don't encourage 'im in 'is impidence."

* " Oh ! " he says a-turnin' on me, " then if you're Mrs. Brown, pray where do you send your children to school ? "

I says, " Where I please."

" Oh ! " he says, " I must know."

I says " Oh ! must you," then I says, " axe about, and find it out, and that's the way to know."

He says, " I'll report you."

I says, " Mind you do, and jest report yourself at the same time for a-impident, intrudin' jackanapes."

He says, " It's 'igh time as somethink were done for to counteract sich ignorance as yours, as is a reg'lar moral pestilence."

" Now," I says, " look 'ere, I ain't a-goin' to stand none of your insults, and if you don't take and walk your chalks, as the sayin' is, in a minit, I'll give you the 'arth broom over your back."

He says, " You shall 'ear more of this."

I says, " And you shall 'ave a taste of this;" and shakes the 'arth broom at 'im.

Poor Miss Lunn, she says, " Oh! pray don't, Mrs. Brown, or you'll frighten ma, and make 'er jump up, as would be down like a sack on all fours, thro' 'er legs a-givin' way."

Well, that fellow, he give a glare and a toss of 'is 'ead, and out of the place he walked, a-sayin' as he'd 'ave me afore a magistrate.

Maria Lunn she werry soon got over it, poor thing, as naturally give 'er a turn, for tho' never married, she were engaged and 'ad 'er weddin' gownd made, over seventeen year to her own first cousin, as were in the Baltic trade, and made over thirty woyages, man and boy, till that one as he never came back from, tho' I have 'eard say as he died a thrivin' man in Canader ; but 'aven't never rote for Maria to jine him out there, nor yet took no notice on 'er, and 'is eldest boy is over sixteen, as was what I calls a base deception to keep up the notion as he were a single man, when he'd been and married another over in Bremen, years and years afore, as were the landlord's daughter, and always come to see Maria arter that with a lie on 'is lips, as the sayin' is, and brought 'er mother

some Danzig sprooce as they calls it, as tasted to
me werry like warm treacle and water with a dash
of turps in it, as they do say is a fine thing for a
inward bruise, but didn't cure poor Maria's broken
'art, as ached for many a long day arter that feller,
and says as she never will believe as he's married
till he tells 'er with 'is own lips, as in course he
can't do in 'is grave, tho' my boy Joe 'as seen 'im
and all the family over there; but in course if it's
any comfort to Maria for to think 'im single, let 'er,
only for my part, I must say as I goes in for morals,
but then you see you can't espect any one in the
Baltic trade for to 'ave the same morals as them as
isn't in it.

But as I told Mrs. Tremlitt, when she were
a-goin' on about that Rooshun religion being nearly
as bad as the Pope, I says, there ain't no fear
of that, for I 'ave 'eard say as them Rooshuns
'ates the Pope quite as much as the Inglish, and
tries to force parties over in Roosher not to believe
in 'im, jest the same as they did used to do in
Ireland.

Not as I've got a word to say agin the Pope
myself, as smiled that pleasant when I see 'im over
in Rome; and as to 'im a settin' on seven 'ills, it's
rubbish, for he couldn't do it no more than any one
else, as certingly did see 'im a-standin' on one myself, as is only a 'uman bein' mortal like the rest on us.

For, as I were a-sayin' only the other day to poor Mrs. Maltby, as 'er lumbager draws double, and in course it's a comfort to know as the Pope's got it, as shows as he's nothink but flesh and blood, the same as the rest on us; tho' I must say as walking in them marble passages, as is like a-leadin' the life of a gallery slave, as the sayin' is, cannot be like the open air for 'im, as is apt to strike you with a chill, and never did think as them flannins as he wears is thick enuf. Yet as I were a-sayin' to Mrs. Maltby, edication's 'umbug, cos, I says, look wot were done in the world afore ever School Boards were 'eard on, and jest look what they did when nobody couldn't rite and read, they never 'ad all the misery as there is now-a-days with every barber's clerk of a feller a-ritin' to a noosepaper.

I'm sure them as is so fond of ritin' might be a-doin' somethink better than a-talkin' the rubbish they do, the same as some old fool as pretends to be a-ritin' from Rome, says as the Pope sets with little sarsers of jewels afore 'im, the same as I've see Barnes 'ave, as were a workin' jeweller, and keeps on a-takin' 'em like pinches of snuff.

A nice state 'is nose would be in if he were to go a-sniffin' up them precious stones, as would soon stuff 'is 'ead up, and work into 'is brain.

A deal of edication there was when Rome were built, as they do say was foundered on seven 'ills, and some says as there's a deal of bad air all about it now.

"No," I says, "Mrs. Maltby, readin' and ritin' won't do parties no good, but," I says, "if this 'ere School Board would learn parties to do their dooty and be decent and sober, and 'ard-workin' that's wot we wants the poor to be and the rich too; and I'm sure there's more bad books rote than good ones; and as to readin', why, wot is it as people in general reads, is it wot will give 'em good morals, and all like that? No, only a lot of rubbish, as turns 'arf the silly gals' and boys' brains, or else some foolery jest to larf at, as is werry well in a general way, but didn't ought to take up too much time always.

I'm sure I never 'ad no time for readin' when I was a gal, but can set and listen now to Brown, as reads to me werry often, and as to Melia Barnes, she's a downright libery she is, as 'ave told me things about 'istory as nobody wouldn't credit, as they could 'ave been that bad all escept Queen Lizzybeth, as were a nat'ral dorter of Old 'Arry, and took after 'er father, as were the father of lies, as Brown always did 'old, and can prove 'is words out of the book; and talk of reformin', I'm sure she never showed no signs on it, and I don't believe if she 'ad been sent to a reformatory as she'd come out any better than she went in, a brazen old 'ussy.

But talk of edication, a deal of good it's done in showin' parties 'ow to forge, and rob, and cheat all the more easier.

Not as I'm ag'in genral information, as is a good thing no doubt in its way, but a deal on it car be picked up 'earsay, as the sayin' is, and I'm sure I've knowed them as never got on at school, turn out that clever arter they left it, as they knowed every thing, and a deal more than they did ought to.

And when you comes for to think it over, wotever is edication but bein' tort all, as everyone else knows, so you're sure to 'ear it sooner or later; not as I believes wot they says in books as may be true, but yet mayn't, 'cos they're nearly all a-guessin', in my opinion.

In course, as I've said afore, you may believe joggraffy, cos there's the places as they can't take away, tho' they changes the names on 'em, like old Beastmark's a-doin' in France, and the same as they're a-doin' with some of the streets at the West End, as makes it werry puzzlin', as is the way as they've been and altered all the numbers of the 'ouses in Gore Street, as is close agin Totten'am Court Road, and I were nicely puzzled a-tryin' to make out the 'ouse were Lady Wittles' sister did used to live, as is over thirty year ago.

But as I were a-sayin', there is somethink to show to prove as joggraffy's true but, as to 'istory, why, any one would be a fool to believe that, when we all knows wot a set of blackguards 'ave rote it, and wot a nice set of willins it's all about, and it's werry easy to set and abuse kings and queens, but as far as I can make out, they've in gen'ral been more fools than knaves, as the sayin' is.

Many on 'em 'as been made use on like tools for a set of waggerbones to rob and murder in the king's name, cos we all knows as kings can't be everywheres, and do everythink theirselves, so must 'ave them under 'em as does the dirty work for 'em, as gets well paid for doin' it; and then these 'ere penny-a-liners, as they calls 'em, takes and rites fine books about 'em, and makes out as they was swells for wirtue, and everythink like that.

Then another lot comes and says they was the wilest of the wile, and that's wot I says about Queen Lizzybeth, you may take and read about 'er, as Brown 'ave done to me scores of times, and the best as 'er friends can say of 'er is as she was a clever, deceitful, lyin' young 'ussey, and then growed to be a wile, artful, nasty, dirty, cruel, rewengeful old devil; for I wouldn't insult the cat by callin' 'er by the same name.

But law, wot do it signify, for arter all wot is she now any more than dust and hashes like the rest on us; but wot I will say is as she ain't 'arf so bad as them as made 'er queen, as she 'adn't no right to be, not because they loved 'er, but only for wot they could get out of 'er, as was sometimes more kicks than 'apence, as the sayin' is; when she was in one of 'er tantrums, and would swear like a bossun in a gale.

But then, look wot some on 'em got out of 'er; why, there was many as wasn't nothink as come to be 'er right 'and, and she give 'em lands and titles, as she'd been and murdered the owners on, like 'Old 'Arry 'er father, and there's some as 'ave got 'em to this day; as is wot puts Brown in such a rage, as says as they took all the property away from the poor and give it to a set of raggermuffins, as is rollin' in riches as they never did nothink for, and as to 'Ospital Sunday, there wouldn't be no heed on it if the poor 'ad thei rights.

And I'm sure it's downright ridiculus 'avin' of that St. George's 'Ospital all among them swell 'ouses, with their balls and parties a-goin' on con stant, and sich a row all night, with a-'ollerin' for carridges, and music a-playin', as must be werry soothin' to them as is a-layin' in their beds preaps a-dyin', or in agony of pain, as wants to get a little sleep, or even a serous thought.

And no doubt if the party as makes up the medsins in some of them 'ospitals puts in a dollop of Prussian acid too much, like the other day, it is thro' 'is 'ead bein' that confused with the row, and it's a 'appy release arter all; tho' some parties says as all the patients in 'ospitals is every one of 'em a-livin' at the rate of 'undreds a year, and might as well be in Belgrave Square, if you comes to reckon up the money as a 'ospital costs to keep up, and the money as is squandered over buildin' 'em, like that there new one over ag'in Westminster Bridge, as did used to stand in the Boro'

But, law bless me, we must all live, and if it wasn't for robbery and cheatin' where should we all be, and that's why it's all kep' up, 'cos if one was to begin to 'oller out they'd all be found out, as is like Chancery, as 'ave been the ruin of millions, as 'ave been and died in the workus and in 'ospitals, let alone them as 'ave been starved and 'ung for stealin', as all the while 'ad got property of their own, as Chancery were a-takin' care on for 'em with a 'ook, and them Lord Chancellors a-rollin' in riches, and so was their clerks; and now I 'ear as this 'ere Gladstin 'ave been and collared the lot, as is millions, and says as he's a-goin' to build new law courts jest outside Temple Bar, but there's some row over it, so they don't go on, as is jest as well; cos, in course, all that money is a-layin' at interest, as brings in thousans every year, and will make the taxes lighter in course; and so it is as they've been able to take the dooty off sugar, as is

a great thing for the poor, as don't get it a penny
cheaper, and I suppose them law courts will be
finished jest the same time as the New Jerusalem is
built, as is wot Mr. Moffat is always a-preachin'
about at 'is Bethesder Chapel, as Mrs. Tremlitt sets
under twice a day of a sabbath, as she calls it, as
I tells 'er she'd better turn Jew at once, as ain't
sich fools as to 'ave 'er, tho' I'm sure she's a reglar
bundle of old clo' as it is.

But, as I says, in course if parties is a-comin'
to your door to ask where you sends your children
to school, the next thing as they'll do will be to
come and ask you where you went to school yourself, or else want you to say your Cattykism afore
Queen Wictorier's Privy Council as they calls it, as
is certingly better than bein' asked them questions,
as preaps you can't anser afore all the congregation
of a Sunday arternoon, as is wot the minister wanted
to do down in the country where Liza lives, and
would 'ave done it too, only the churchwarden
wouldn't let 'im, as brought on words in the westry,
as ended in 'em not a-carryin' the church-rate.

But any'ow I don't mean to be took at a non-
plush, so wot with wot I've 'eard and wot I've
read, I'm pretty well up in readin', ritin', and rith-
metic, tho' as to the use of the globes I'm quite at
a standstill myself, tho' in course I knows what
joggraphy means, and as to 'istory, I've reglar got

it at my fingers' end, thro' a-knowin' as Queen Anne
is dead, as never could get over the death of 'er
mother, Mary Queen of Scots, not as she 'ad any
'and in it, but yet the thought on it give 'er them
constant low sperrits as they do say drove her to
drinkin', the same as poor Mrs. Trimlett, as were
never a woman as any one ever see turn a 'air, as
the sayin' is, till 'er two sons listed in one day, and
couldn't buy 'em off, as she said she never would consent to, tho' not a woman to fly in Queen Wictorier's
face, nor yet take 'er shillin' and then deny it, but yet
that objection to the army thro' 'avin' a uncle in the
Marines as married a black woman in Barbadoes, as
fust brought dissensions into the family thro' beiu'
a Methodist, and all 'er family that strict to their
Church, with a family wault and iron railin's sacred
to the memory of 'er own grandfather, as were a fell-
monger in Bermondsey, and the churchwarden 'ad
took down thro' not bein' kep' up in decent repair,
as is a wiolation of the dead, the same as old St.
Pancris Church-yard as that new railroad runs
over, as is a disgraceful sight in my opinion, tho' in
course the dead must make way for the livin', as is
the way of the world; but yet you don't like to see
your family-grave reglar destroyed afore you can be
laid in it yourself as is your rights, and no knowin'
when you may want it, not as I cares for a brick
wault and berried in lead like a tea - chest

myself, as in my opinion "ashes to ashes, dust to dust," is the nat'ral way, accordin' to the decay of natur.

I've been a-lookin' over a lot of 'istory books, as is called Pinnicks, and Mrs. Markem, and Goldsmith, and a good many more, as is rather confusin', cos you can't tell as they knowed anythink about it, but 'as only rote like me, jest wot they've 'eard say, but as far as I can make out it's always the same story, all a-cuttin' of one another's throats for wot they can get out of 'em; and a-lyin' and a-stealin' all round; and a-callin' of theirselves Christians all the time, as was nice speciments of the article from Julia Seizer downwards, not as he were so bad as many as come arter him; for I'm sure the more I reads the more I stares to think of wot 'ave been done, as in my opinion it would be a deal better not to have no 'istory, like the Merrykins, for it's only a bad esample for young people to read sich things in books, and that's why I'm agin edication, as is only a-puttin' parties up to them bad ways, as is wot their forefathers give into, and I'm sure if my grandfather 'ad been King George the Fourth, and could 'ave be'aved as bad as he did to my grandmothers, I'd 'ave drored a wail over 'is mem'ry, not as they 'ave put up no descriptions on 'im anywheres under 'is slattys, tho' they may on 'is tombstone, not as ever I see it tho' he's berried in Winsor; but never

shall respect 'is mem'ry, tho' preaps arter all he
ain't 'arf as black as he's painted.

But in course we must go with the times, as the
sayin' is.

So I'm a-readin', for I ain't a-goin' to cut a bad
figger afore the School Board when I gets summonsed afore 'em, tho' they may dodge me with
some of their off-'and questions, yet I shall be able to
'old my own and give 'em as good as they brings,
and as to them stuck-up 'umbugs as asks me questions about Roosher,—

I've got my anser, as they may read in
welcome.

I don't think as ever I should 'ave give that
royal marriage a second thought, as the sayin' is,
but for thinkin' so much over ow Queen Wictorier
would like a-bein' mixed up with them Rooshuns, as
is terrible bears I've 'eard say; besides, not bein'
used to their ways and not a-likin' to see parties a-
goin' about in nothing but a sheep-skin, nor yet
drink raw sperrits every minit to keep the cold out,
and then preaps have 'er own son get a touch of the
nout as they calls it, or sent over to Siberier, as is
where the crabs comes from, as ain't over whole-
some, yet jest picked is pretty eatin', but requires
a onion and plenty of ile, and then in my opinion,
lighter than a lobster. I'm sure when Brown come
in and told me as Queen Wictorier 'erself were a-goin'

over to Petersbug for to see that there son of 'ern married, it give me quite a turn, tho' in course she must give 'im away, as she might do by letter.

I says to 'im, I says, " Then in my opinion it didn't ought to be allowed."

He says, " Why not ? "

I says, " Why not, indeed ; why, a good many nots, I should say, for wot do we know about them Rooshuns as we should take and trust them with our Queen, as it's only the other day as we was a-fightin' with 'em."

" Well," says Brown, " wot of that, we're at peace with 'em now."

" Yes," I says, " I knows that, but 'ow do we know but what they mightn't take and break the peace and go to war with us the werry moment as they've got Queen Wictorier in their power, as might end her days, poor dear, shut up in a icebug."

Brown, he says, " Oh ! it ain't no use a-talkin' to you."

" No," I says, " and it ain't no use me a-talkin' to others, cos they don't follow my advice, as if they 'ad things might 'ave been werry different, and never no war with Roosher; not as that mat- ters now, as it's all over ; but," I says, " depend on it, it's all some of that Gladstin's tricks, a-gettin' Queen Wictorier to go over there, cos in course he can do as he likes the moment as 'er back is turned, cos when the cat's away the mice'll play, as the sayin' is, and we shall 'ave 'im a-goin' to war with every one, and a nice bill we shall 'ave to pay for it all, as is always the way when you leaves 'ome, and 'as a bill at a shop; for I'm sure that time as I went to Margit for a fortnight, and left Mrs. Cartlet and 'er 'usban' to take care of the 'ouse, the bill they run up for me at Mrs. Tottel's, as is the chandlery shop, were enuf to make your 'air stand on end, as the sayin' is, and everything put down under firewood and black-lead, with 'arth-stones and bath-bricks throwed in with soap and soda, as really meant pickles, and tea and sugar too, no doubt; but 'owever could I pick 'em out, and say wot were wot?

So it is when we 'as a bill come in for a war; whoever is to look it over, and 'owever can Queen Wictorier check it, as can't tell 'ow many guns was wanted, nor yet 'ow much gunpowder were used, let alone the food for them sojers and their boots a-runnin' into a fortin'; not as their clothes can cost much, if they pays for them as they do the shirts, as it's three-'apence a-piece they gives to poor women to make 'em, as is that coarse work as wears the fingers to the bone, as the sayin' is; and 'ave knowed them as was born ladies drove thro' want to take that work; so depend on it, if Queen Wictorier goes to Roosher, there'll be nice Meg's diversions at 'ome, while 'er back's turned; cos tho' in course she'll leave them Ministers on board wages, they'll pitch into everythink nicely when she's gone, cos in course she can't lock up every place, and take all them keys along with 'er, as must weigh 'undreds, for Win'sor Castle must be full of closets, let alone the other places as she do frequent, as must take up all 'er time a-packin' and unpackin', I should think, let alone that travellin' by night with your rest broke into; and I'm sure it is our dooties for to 'rite and beg on 'er not to trust 'erself among them Rooshun bears, as Miss Pilkinton were a-readin' about at Mrs. Padwick's, the other day, and of all the wretches as ever I did 'ear on, they're the wust, a-darin' for to christen them young hinfants thro' a hole cut in the ice, and a-lettin' 'em slip thro' the minister's fingers a-freezin', as takes it that cool when one falls into the 'ole, as for to say, " That one's gone—give me another;' as I considers murder in cold blood with a wengeance, as the sayin' is.

And whyever can't they 'ave the ice thawed proper, but not with puttin' a red-ot poker to the pipes, as were wot our gal did, two winters ago, with my back turned, and every pipe busted at the werry spot when the thaw come, and both kitchens flooded back and front, as certingly were enuf to make any one swear, tho' Brown's langwidge did give me the creeps, as went down in the dark, and

were over 'is ankles without 'is shoes, for to fetch
up the lucifers as we'd left on the kitchen table, and
didn't remember till we woke, just about two, and
wanted to see the time, so as to call the gal, and
'ave 'is breakfast ready by six, thro' a-goin' off by
the train at seven, with a cab ordered overnight,
and couldn't find 'is slippers in the dark, as 'ad
been put in 'is bag, a-thinkin' he wouldn't want,
cos he'd put on 'is boots the fust thing in gettin'
up.

But, as I were a-sayin', jest fancy Queen Wictorier up in Roosher, and couldn't be got at, and
that Gladstin a-comin' some of his games, and sent
to the Tower, as in course she could do by the
telegraft to the Lord Mare, but not sign 'is death-
warrant the same as Queen Lizzybeth did to Mary
Queen of Scots, and yet a-pretendin' as she never
done it only by a mistake; as is wot that gal Liza
Trimmins said when I found my welwet cape and a
lace square in 'er box, but wouldn't do for me; not
as I'd give 'er in charge, cos in course they'd 'ave
took and 'quitted 'er; so I says to the perlice as
come in, " Let 'er go ;" tho' he did say as I were
a compounded felony, and a-condolin' with the
offence, as was werry bad langwidge to use to me
in my own front kitchen, as in course that gal and
'er mother took advantage on, and talked of 'avin'
the law of me.

I were so put out at 'earin' of Queen Wictorier a-goin' to them outlandish parts, and as I were a-goin' to 'ave a cup of tea with Mrs. Padwick, thought as I'd mention it to a party as lodges with 'er, and is a Swedenborgin, as is somewheres near Roosher, and quite as cold, and believes as wotever you do in this world you'll 'ave to do in the next, as is a bad look-out for perlicemen, as is out all weathers, and them as stands at the wash-tub all day, let alone sweeps and scavengers, as isn't jobs as I should care about for ever and ever, any more than a stoker or a ingin-driver; but in course parties a-sayin' as they believe things don't make 'em true, any more as that there Dr. Cumming, as 'ave fixed the day for the end of the world over and over agin, and goes to bed with 'is things on, for fear of bein' called up in the middle of the night, and never don't allow no dinner to be ordered for to-morrer, and begrudges new clothes for 'is family, and won't 'ave the 'ouse painted, and, when the things goes to the wash, never espects to see 'em back agin.

But, law, it is quite wonderful wot people do say now-a-days, for Miss Pilkinton she were a-tellin' me as she'd been a-'earin' of a party preach at St. Paul's as knowed all about wot 'appened afore Adam and Eve was born or thought of.

So I says, " 'Owever could he know that?"

She says, "Oh, there's wonderful things found out, all thro' a stone as they've been and picked up in the desert, all 'rote over, as they says did once belong to them Moerbites, as lived afore Moses."

"Law," I says, "'ow singler to 'rite on stones, escept it were tombstones, as in course would prove anyone's death, leastways their berrial;" not as you can believe wot is 'rote about parties on their tombstones, cos if we was 'arf as good in life as we are in death, this world would be full of lovin' fathers and faithful wives, and children as was angels, and all deeply lamented with mournin' their untimely ends.

"Well," she says, "this 'ere Moerbite stone may 'ave been a tombstone, tho' some says as other Moerbites 'rote all about theirselves on it, and dropped it as they went along."

"Ah," I says, "the same as parties at sea 'rites things in a bottle, and throws 'em overboard, as is sometimes a 'oax, as is a werry 'artless one, and wot led to poor Mrs. Malin's sister in the name of Tripley a-goin' to church with that man Yallerton, as swore as Tripley 'ad gone down with the 'Golden Land,' bound for 'Ong Kong, and every soul perished, as were all picked up in this bottle, as turned up at the werry church door as they was a-comin' out, so in course claimed 'is wife; not but wot she'd a lucky escape, for that feller were a waggerbone,

and only arter 'er money; and Tripley never went
to sea no more, but lived to berry 'er and two more
arter 'er, as reads werry affectin', all three on one
tombstone, as is why I don't think much of wot's
put on a tombstone, not whether it's a Moerbite or
not, cos I dessay they was, like Tripley and the rest
of the world, werry soon reconciled to their loss,
as the sayin' is; and as to 'im a-considerin' them
three wives angels, why, they lived cats' and dogs'
lives, as the sayin' is; and no doubt he were glad
enuf to put anythink on their tombstone, so long
as he could put them under it; as weren't a character as I cared about, cos I don't 'old with a man
a-marryin' agin the day arter 'is wife's funeral, as
ain't a-treatin' of 'er memory with respect, wotever
he may 'ave put on 'er tombstone about 'afflicshun
sore, long time I bore,' as don't come from the 'art,
and is only a 'oller mockery, the same as 'oldin' a
'ankercher to the mouth, as won't stop no real tears
a-flowin', but may 'ide a smile, as is wot I calls
double-faced ways.

But, as I were a-sayin', this 'ere Rooshun marriage me and Mrs. Padwick got a-talkin' over it,
and both on us agreed as Gladstin were at the
bottom on it, and I says, "It do aggrawate me to
see any one put upon like that, tho' she is our sufferin'
lady we all knows, and sich a dear good soul as Queen
Wictoïer, as took and give the werry shawl off her

7

back to a poor old 'Ighlander as she see a-workin'
out in the wet, not as they minds it them Scotch,
cos they don't pay no attentions to the rains any
more than if it wasn't nothink a-comin' down on
'em, as the werry children will take and play in it
without no shoes nor stockins on.

But Queen Wictorier a-sendin' that poor old
man in the rain 'er werry own shawl shows a very
different sperrit to Queen 'Lizzybeth, as wouldn't
step over a puddle without one of them lords a-
layin' down 'is cloak for 'er to walk over it, and if
he 'adn't a-done it she'd 'ave took and tore it off
'is back, and then 'ad 'is 'ead off in a brace of
shakes, as the sayin' is; but Queen Wictorier ain't
Queen 'Lizzybeth, thank goodness, or there would
be a row.

As I says to Mrs. Padwick, I says, "Any one
did ought to 'ave the stomich of a 'orse, as the
sayin' is, to be able to eat them Rooshun messes,
as I 'ave 'eard say as they never takes their soup
till it stood to get sour, as will turn in a night with
wegetables in; and as to drinkin', we all knows as
train-ile is their fancies, as they will 'ave even if
they 'as to drain the lamps for to get it, as left Paris
in total darkness thro' a-drinkin' up all the street
lamps in one night, as shows as we did ought to be
thankful for gas, as, tho' it do smell unpleasint, it
can't never be drunk up, tho' it may be cut off if

you don't pay your rates, like the water; and my dear mother remembers quite well afore it come in, as wasn't till there were a Regent thro' old King George bein' shet up, for he were that obstinate as he wouldn't never 'ave allowed it, cos in course it did a dreadful deal of 'arm to the ilemen, and reglar run 'em off the road, the same as railways 'as the stage-coaches.

"Oh," says Mrs. Padwick, "it's a pity as tho Dook of Wellin'ton ain't alive, he'd never 'ave let 'er go to no Rooshers, as aint a safe place, cos jest look 'ow they took and served Old Boney when he went, as went a-meanin' to stop all the winter with 'em, and was reglar burnt out of 'is bed the fust night, as is wot you wouldn't espect to be in Roosher, as is all frost and snow; so," I says, "if I was the Prince of Wales, I should say, 'Ma, dear, you 'adn't better wenture;' and yet would be orkard for 'im, cos in course Alfred would up, and say, 'I considers that mean in you, Wales, as 'ad mother at your weddin', and now begrudges me 'avin' of 'er at mine,' as would bring on words, as them Rooshuns would only be too glad to ferment the quarrel, cos, in course, they can't never forgive wot we done to 'em in the Crimeer, at sendin' em a charge of six 'undred thousand, with Lord Cardigin at their 'ead, tho' not wot we 'ad to pay the 'Merrykins, but were too 'eavy a charge for them all

the same, tho' we did call it the light brigade; but
that were our art jest to throw 'em off their guards,
as is often done in war, I've 'eard say, and considered all fair, the same as when you're in love;
but I'm sure there ain't no love lost between
us and the Rooshuns, and if they could set
all the Royal Family by the ears they would be
glad.

Not but Queen Wictorier's too much the lady to
'ave any low-lived rows over a weddin' or a funeral
either, as I 'ave knowed 'appen, as is 'ow old
Mrs. Flinn got 'er eye knocked out with the 'andle
of a pint pot when they berried Flinn; and it's all
rubbish of Mrs. O'Dowd to tell me as she reglar
cried it out, as in course is only all my eye, as the
sayin' is.

They do say as it's a werry good match for 'im,
thro' 'er bein' that rich; but, law, we don't want
none of them forriners' money, as never can buy
our 'arts; and I'm sure we all loves that there
Princess of Wales the same tho' she 'adn't nothink
but wot we give 'er, poor dear, and as welcome to
it as flowers in spring, as the sayin' is.

Well, we was a-chattin' away, me and Mrs.
Padwick, and she says, "Martha Brown, your
cold's werry 'eavy on your chest."

I says, "Right you are, as am goin 'ome early,
and means to 'ave a onion porridge for my

with my feet in a pail of 'ot water up to my knees,
and a taller plaister on my chest."

So I wouldn't stop to 'ave black-puddin's along
with 'er, and baked taters, as does like balls of
flour in 'er Dutch-oven; but 'ome I goes, and 'as a
bit of fire in my bed-room, plenty of 'ot water, and
some 'ot rum-and-water with a lump of butter in
it, as I were a-goin' to drink the last thing afore
gettin' into bed, as the gal brought it me up a-
steamin', and puts it down by my side as I were
a-settin' with towels over the fender for to dry
my feet.

I says, " You needn't set up for your master ;"
cos I would never 'ave no servant a-callin' 'im
Mr. Brown nor me Mrs. Brown to my face.

So I says, " Your master won't be in till late ;
so go to bed."

I felt as that warm water were a-drorin' out my
cold, and drunk down my rum-and-water, and 'ad
got the towel in my 'and, when I looks up, and
there were Brown, as 'ad come in like a mouse for
quietness, tho' he would 'ave it as I were fast
asleep with my feet in 'ot water, and the place
a-smellin' of rum enuf to pison any one.

So I says, " Rum won't never pison you, my
pippin, for you've took enuf on it to prove that, and
as to the place a-smellin' on it, I were jest a-goin'
to take the least as is, afore gettin' into bed."

He says, " You've been and mopped up the lot, but," he says, " as you've got the 'ot water, I'll 'ave a drop myself," and so he did, thro' a feelin' chilly.

He says, " It's a pity as you've got sich a bad cold, Martha, cos," he says, " I were a-goin' to ask you if you'd like to 'ave a run over to forrin parts along o' me, as am off to Po next Thursday."

I says, " Wherever is Po ?" I says.

" Why," he says, " over in France, as am a-goin' over to see about this 'ere trackshun break, and I thought as you'd like to come."

" Oh ! yes," I says, " Brown, for I do want a bit of a change, and," I says, " should like for to see Paris agin arter them Petrolines 'ave been at their games, and," I says, " I should like to 'ave a somethink done to my teeth over there, as is werry clever with your teeth, I've 'eard say, as is more than them adwertisin' dentists is in the general way, tho' some on 'em may be honest and do their dooty by your mouth, when they takes it in 'and ; and if they don't wherever is your remedy, for as to law, why, the remedy is wuss than the disease, as the sayin' is, not as I'd speak agin all dentists, cos we all knows as there ain't no rule without a deception, and as to that man over my teeth, he were a reglar mask of deception and as false as the teeth in the case at 'is door. But where are you to trust any one, and I'm sure I never will agin, arter the friend I were to that thief, young Chalks, tho' as to the law, I often 'ave said, and will say it agin, as I'd rather be trampled under foot, like the ox in the grass, as the sayin' is, than go to law with anybody or anythink, as I'm sure I paid that thief of a feller, as I'd employed about the place, that five pounds into the County Court, as was like payin' of my own money over agin, for I'd trusted 'im to pay a few bills for me, and says to 'im, " Take the money out of the drawer, thro' bein' up to my elbers in starchin', and he knowed where I put it, thro' 'im 'avin' jest got a Post-office order changed for me, and thought as I could 'ave trusted 'im thro' bein' own brother to Mrs. Dimlock, as is in the stationery line, and 'ad been out o' work for months, no doubt through 'is pilferin' ways.

So I give 'im a job at cleanin' winders, and washed all the paint down for me, and 'adn't a fardin' to bless 'imself with, and not a meal to put in 'is 'ead, but wot I give 'im, and then to turn round after a year and a 'arf, and say as he'd adwanced that money for me, as 'adn't 'ardly a shoe to 'is foot, a waggerbone, but I paid the money into court, as 'll come 'ome to 'im some day, and won't never do 'im no good, a ungrateful, good-for-nothink thief, as they tells me 'ave took to the sea, as is all as he's fit for, a waggerbone.

But when it come to that there dentist a-puttin'

me and my teeth in the County Court, it were more
than flesh and blood could put up with, so I says,
"I'll defend it to my last drop," and did so, accordin', and down at that Court, by 'arf-past nine
to be there at the openin'; but law, no more use
than stoppin' in bed, for a party as were summonsed
with a donkey cart, as she had to pay off by the
week, got afore me, and the fendin' and provin'
as there were, kep' me till they went to get their
lunches, and I never come up for judgment till jest
on the stroke of three.

I ain't got a word to say agin that judge, nor
not nobody else about that Court, tho' I must say
as that lawyer as asked me a lot of questions made
'isself werry ridiculous?

For he says, "Mrs. Brown, mum, do you re-
collect when you fust 'ad your teeth?"

I says, "I will speak the truth, and not go to
deceive no one, and cannot say as I do, tho' I well
remembers my dear mother a-sayin'——"

Says the Judge, "Was your mother with you?"

I says, "Oh dear, yes! my lord, for a better
mother never lived in this world, and 'ave 'eard 'er
say as it took 'er and both 'er married sisters to
'old me when fust I 'ad my gums launched."

Says that lawyer, "Who launched your gums?"

"Why," I says, "I believe it were Mr. Portlock,
who attended my dear mother with 'er fust seven."

"What are you talkin' about ?" says the Judge. "Do you mean your mother's fust seven teeth ?"

"No," I says, "children, and as to teeth, I've 'eard 'er say I were that for'ard with mine as to bite 'er finger till the blood come, within six months, tho' only four through top and bottom."

Says the lawyer, "We don't want to 'ear about your fust teeth, but are a-talkin' about them as you ordered of my client."

I says, "Then whyever go back to when I fust 'ad my teeth ?"

"He meant your false teeth," says the Judge.

I says, "Then, why not say so? tho' I thanks you, my Lord, for a-mentionin' of it, for I'm one as anyone can lead with a kind word, but steam-injins can't drive."

He says, "Well, then, did you order these teeth ?"

I says, "Certingly not ; as is nothink better than misfits, and shouldn't think of payin' that price for 'em, not to 'ave things rammed into my mouth, as is for all the world like bein' gagged, and couldn't speak plain, let alone eat my wittles, as is wot one nat'rally espects in teeth ; and as to a-settin' off my mouth, why, they stuck that for'ard, jest for all the world as if I was a-spittin' 'em out, and not a bit like a lovely picter I've see of a 'ansome young woman, as looked like 'er own grandmother, with 'er teeth out, tho' quite the gal agin when replaced, as is wot fust put it in my 'ead to 'ave 'em."

Says the lawyer, "My client never 'ad no sich picter about 'is place."

I says, "I never said as he 'ad; but what does that signify? Teeth is teeth all the world over, and so is the 'uman 'ead, tho' I 'ave 'eard speak of a party as lived out somewhere Black'eath way, as 'ad a double row like a crockerdile, as I should say wouldn't look well in the 'uman mouth."

Says the Judge, "You don't deny orderin' the teeth?"

I says, "Certingly not; but they was to be self-adjustin', with patent springs, and not 'arf-a-mile too big for my mouth, as would come out like a mask of bone with me only givin' a smile; and as to yawnin', I'm werry sure, if I 'ad wentured so far, as lock-jaw would be the consequence."

"I think," says the Judge, a-yawnin' 'isself, "as you might settle this matter out of court; and I'm sure, Mrs. Brown, as this gentleman will make your teeth fit you to a nicety."

I says, "It's impossible, without cuttin' away a bit of my jaw, as is a thing as I won't submit to, for I knows werry well wot comes of that, thro' 'avin' my bannisters cut away for to make room for the back door to open proper, as all give way with me, and pitched me 'ead-fust down the kitchen-stairs, as would 'ave been my death if, as luck would 'ave it, I 'adn't shet the tail of my gownd in the back-door, as 'eld me tight thro' it a-bangin' to with the thoro' draft."

"Well, then," says the Judge, "you'll agree?" I says, "Certingly, when I knows wot it is." Says the Judge, "Call the next case."

"But——" I says.

"Step this way," says a officer, a-touchin' me on the harm.

So I follers 'im into another room, and there I 'ad to pay a somethink for fees, and see that lawyer, as said it were all settled as I should 'ave the teeth fitted in proper, and pay the money a pound a month, as were wot I'd agreed to afore the Judge.

I'm sure I never 'adn't agreed to nothink of the sort; but, law! there's no copin' with them lawyers, nor yet with dentists neither; tho' I must say in the end as he did make somethink of a job of them teeth, tho' it were months afore I could tackle my cracklin' with comfort, and as to filberts, I aint 'ad the pluck to try 'em yet. "So," I says, "when next in Paris, I'll 'ave 'em looked to." But, law! I might as well be a-talkin' to the bed-post, for Brown he'd took 'is drop of somethink 'ot, and were a-snorin' like a porpus.

So up I gets, and says, "I must be a-gettin' ready for startin'," but still 'ad my 'ead

a-runnin' on this 'ere Rooshun marridge, as I'd
dreamt about over and over agin, thro' a-feelin'
that ankshus as things should go right thro'
'avin' of my misgivin's, for I'm one of them
'eavy dreamers, I am, as seems to foretell things
like, and in course I aint nobody to the Royal
Family, nor them to me, and that's why I can't for
the life of me think whyever Queen Wictorier should
'aunt me so in my dreams about 'er family, not as I
means to deny a feelin' of that interested about 'em
as makes me 'ope this marridge may turn out
better than I espects; and there's a many more
besides me as shakes their heads over it, but arter
all it's better as he should marry anyone as he likes
than anyone as he don't, and he certingly 'ave 'ad
plenty to choose from thro' 'avin' been that traveller,
not in course as he could 'ave took any one over in
Horsetralia, nor yet Ameriker, cos the young gal
might be all werry well 'erself, but then there'd
'ave been the family, as aint werry often quite up to
the knocker, as the sayin' is, in them wild parts."

Not but what he could 'ave got plenty of money
if he'd 'ave took a wife out of them Ingin princes,
but that wouldn't never 'ave done, cos they'd 'ave
wanted 'im to 'ave 'ad a dozen or two, as is what
Queen Wictorier wouldn't never 'ave stood, not for
all the gold of the Hinges, as the sayin' is.

I could not get that notion of Queen Wictorier

a-wenturin' of 'er precious self among them Rooshuns,
as must be a wild, froze-up lot, and I don't believe
as all the roppin' up in the world will keep you
from ketchin' cold, if you esposes yourself the same
as that night with me and Brown a-goin' over to
Paris by the mail, as I were that ropped up with
fleecy osery and two flannin petticoats, and a
knitted jacket under my linsey gown, and then one
of them clouds over my 'ead, bonnet and all, and
two thick shawls tied round me that tight as I
couldn't draw my breath for 'em; and I'm sure when
I got into the railway carridge and fell back in my
seat, I couldn't never 'ave got up agin but for them
straps as 'angs by the winders, as I pulled out two of
them by the roots, and reg'lar rolled out of the train
at Dover, and 'ad to go sideways down the gangway
with one sailor a-guidin' and the other a-pushin' me
gentle, and all the way across never moved from the
one spot as I'd dropped into on deck as soon as I
got aboard, and don't believe as ever I should 'ave
landed at Cally, if it 'adn't been as a Frenchman as
were follerin' me up the gangway, 'adn't took and
lost 'is temper cos he couldn't pass me, and give me
that wiolent shove as made two of them Johndarms
take my part, and pull me on to the peer, as the railway 'ad run on to, and got me into the carridge,
with them 'ot water things in the bottom of the
carridge, as seemed to burn my feet and not to

warm 'em, for it were a bitter cold night, and only one other besides me and Brown in the carridge as were a forrinner in a fur coat in the corner.

We was soon off and a-rushin' on to Paris, and I set there ever so long and a-listenin' to the others a-snorin', when all of a suddin' I looks up and there set Queen Wictorier afore me, that muffled up, as says to me, a-smilin' grashus, "You see, Mrs. Brown, there aint no fear of me a-takin' cold any more than you, and only 'opes as that lamp won't drip over our 'eads."

I says, "Your Majesty is no doubt illudin' to the ile, as I 'opes you won't never put your royal lips to."

She give a shiver and says, "I 'ave 'eard speak of Roosher bein' cold, but this is a stinger."

"Yes," I says, "and with my cold a-clingin' to me, it seems to strike to me, and seems so odd not to let any one wear shoes and stockin's."

"Oh!" she says, "it aint the ticket."

"Oh!" I says, "indeed, but wot is the sense of bein' ropped up all over your 'ead and your feet a-freezin'"

"Ah!" she says, "that's wot I told my boy when he set 'is 'art on 'avin' of 'er."

"Well," I says, "mum, you've been lucky in your sons and dorters too, as is no doubt thro' bein' that indulgent ma."

"Ah!" she says, "I always likes to be a mother to every one, and look arter everythink myself, as is the best plan."

"Ah," I says, "right you are, and I'm glad to 'ear it, for," I says, "my good gentleman always says ''umbug' when he sees in the papers as you've been grashus pleased to appint a Commisshun for to look into things, and certingly I must say as them Commisshuners of the Common Shores aint much use down our way, and if any time you was a-passin' you'd jest look into our drains, you'd see as they wasn't laid proper, as in course overfloods the place arter a 'eavy rain, as brings on fevers, the same as your own royal eldest 'ad, with a nice narrer squeak for 'is life, as the sayin' is."

" Why," says she, "if you don't like Commishuns, you don't like Boards."

I says, " Like Boards indeed, I should think not, cos look at this 'ere School Board a-comin' and a-pryin' into parties' private affairs, and in my opinion that there Parlyment is no good, and don't believe much in a jury, and that's why I 'olds with the Rooshuns, as I remember a-'earin' about that time as the Hemperor's pallis were burnt down, and 'im a-turnin' round and a-sayin', 'Who'll undertake to build it up agin by this time twel month,' and a party a-steppin' forard and sayin', 'I'll do it.' "

" ' All right,' says the Hemperor, ' but mind it's

done, and no mistake;' and built it were, and that
party as done it got lots of money by the job, but if
he'd 'ave failed, why, he'd 'ave got the 'nout if not the
gallus, and," I says, "if you was to act like that by
Gladstin and them fellers, they wouldn't dare make
them mulls over bringin' in their bills, and then say it
were Parlyment as was to blame; but," I says, "do
you think as it's Parlyment's fault as things is so
dear, cos if so, I'm sure if I was you I'd dis-
solve it.

"And I must say as I do consider as them
Yankees ain't got nothink to 'owl over in this
Virginius, cos in course if a vessel full of fellers was
to come and land in Ireland for to turn it into a reglar
Merrykin rowdy place, why, in course you'd jest
say to your cousin, 'George, there's a dear, jest
step over to Ireland and give them Merrykin 'umbugs
a good lickin', and send em 'back with more stripes
than stars a good deal, and not stand no 'umbug of
a Commishun a-goin' over to set upon it somewhere.'

"And now I am on the subject, your grashus
Majesty, whyever 'ave you gone and let that Gladstin 'ave a war with them niggers, cos as to slaves,
why, it's a mussy to take them poor creeturs away
from them others as would 'eat 'em; only in course
it did ought to be done proper, and not 'uddle 'em
up in a wessel as ain't seaworthy, like some of our

poor hemigrants, as is sent off like pigs, to be drowned into the bargin."

I see as Queen Wictorier were a-beginnin' to nod 'er royal 'ead, as I thought were 'er way when she didn't want to anser, so I changes the subjec, and says, " Do you think as that there Disraly would suit you better ? "

She didn't say a word, but only give a wink, as meant somethink.

" Well," I says, " for my part, I've always found them Jews warm friends myself, and I'm sure I'd trust Mrs. Israels with untold gold thro' a-knowin' 'er to be that 'onest as brought me back a farden as she'd found in the bottom of my Joe's trowsers as she'd bought of me second'and, and I do believe would 'ave brought it all the same if it 'ad been a sovrin, and," I says, " I'm sure any time as your Majesty 'ave got any left worn apparel, she'll do you justice, and always brought me that passover bread and a bit of almond puddin', and little things like that, as shows a thoughtful disposition when you're a-feastin' yourself to think of a naybour.

" But," I says, " I am glad to think as that young Prince Leopold is gettin' that strong, tho' in my opinion you lets 'im go about too much, as did ought to lead a more quieter life, not but it must be quiet enuf up in Scotland, but if he's a fidgety disposition,

why, it's no use a-tryin' to keep 'im in now as he's
growed up, cos they won't be treated like children,
I always says it's no use bein' that stric when
they comes to 'ave whiskers, but," I says, "'owever
your Majesty can stand this 'ere cold, why," I says,
"I'm a-dyin' on it, and," I says, "it's so dark too,
and," I says, "I do believe as there's a bear a-
settin' behind you."

"Oh!" she says, "I'm used to the cold and bears
too, for," she says, "if you only knowed wot I've 'ad
to put up with from that there Gladstin, as is that
temper, as a bear with a sore 'ead is a fool to 'im."

"Well then," I says, "mum, why not sack the
lot? not but wot it's much use a-changin'."

"Oh! no," she says, "and a nice choice I've got,
cos it's not only me, but Parlyment as 'ave to be
sooted."

I says, "I'm sure I shouldn't stand none of their
cheek, and why not do without 'em the same as
Gladstin 'ave in a-goin' to war with these 'ere niggers as lives on the Gold Coast, as is in course why
they're a-goin' to 'ave their 'eads punched; cos," I
says, "as to slavery, your Majesty, it's all my eye,
cos we never said a word to the Merrykins when
they 'ad slaves, and if they was to 'ave 'em agin we
shouldn't dare to 'ave no war with 'em over it, but
can blaze away at them niggers as ain't got no
clothes on to purtect 'em.

"Not," I says, "but that there Gladstin is a deep un too, for he's took jolly good care not to send them as knows all about them nigger parts, as would settle it all in a brace of shakes, as the sayin' is, but," I says, "I do 'ope as you don't let 'im gammon you too much?"

She only give a smile, as much as to say, I knows my way about, thank you.

So, I says, "You'll escuse me, your Majesty, but," I says, "I do 'ope as you won't have no bal-dykinos put up; tho' it certingly would be 'andy over you 'ead in Roosher."

She says, "There's many a slip twixt the cup and the lip."

I says, "That's true, and I feels a-slippin' now, and my feet that awful cold, as I do believe this 'ere 'ot water thing 'ave took and froze, and," I says, "preaps it's their Rooshun ways, to rub your feet in ice to warm 'em, the same as they does your nose and ears when frostbit in Canader."

And I says, "When we gets to Roosher, I do 'ope as you won't go a-slidin' nor a skatin', as would fall 'eavy like myself, and I do 'ope as you won't go a-trustin' them Rooshuns too far, and if your son is a-goin' to live over there 'arf the year, why, mind it's the best 'arf, and 'ave 'im 'ome for Christmas time, as will be a nice escuse to say a you likes to 'ave 'em all round you."

And I says, "Now as we are tiled, as the sayin' is, if I was you I should jest look into things a little more, for you're a deal too easy, you are, indeed; and thro' a-doin' right yourself thinks as every one is the same; but, mark my words, things ain't a-goin' that square as they did ought to be, and when you gets back from Roosher it'll be a werry good time for you to 'aul 'em over the coals, as no doubt you'll find as they've been a-burnin' jest as if they was down agin to even money, as the sayin' is; but," I says, "remember as the frost breaks up werry suddin in Roosher, and they rings a bell to warn you."

Jest then I 'eard a wiolent ringin', and I says, "Lay 'old of me, your Majesty, for 'ere's the thaw, and this 'ere place as we're a-standin' on is a-givin' way under our werry feet, as is ice; so," I says, "pray, let's come indoors, for I'm sure you'll get your royal death, and so shall I."

And jest then I tries to move, and felt as the earth were a-givin' way with me.

I says, "Run, your Majesty, for your life," I says; "pray, do, that's a dear soul, for," I says, "the ice is a-breakin' up suddin, and we shall both be drownded," and I says, "ketch 'old of me."

I were jest a-goin' to take 'er royal 'and, when that bear as I'd see in the corner, come behind er and me, jest atween us,

I made a rush for to save 'er from 'im, when the ice under my feet give way, and down I went, and must 'ave gone altogether, if that bear 'adn't cort me in 'is arms.

I'd jest time to say it's all up with me, and give a wiolent plunge as seemed to kick all the world from under my feet, and I give a scream, and tried to get away from that bear, as says to me, " Be quiet, you old fool, or you'll break your legs over the pail," and took and set me down, and struck a lucifer, and if it wasn't Brown in 'is new rough coat as he's got for travellin'

So I says, " Why, you've been 'ome 'ours ago."

He says, " Jest come."

And he says, " Martha, I really mustn't go away, and leave you alone; why, you must be off your chump, a-settin' 'ere in the dark, with your legs in a pail of cold water."

I says, " Why, wotever time is it?"

He says, " Jest on two."

" Why," I says, " then I've been a-settin' in that pail since ten, as is when I sent the gal to bed, so must 'ave fell asleep, and never took my 'ot rum-and-water for my cold."

" Oh! yes," he says, " you did when I come in, for here's the empty tumbler."

I says, " I've got my churchyarder then, for my toes is all benumbed," and so they was, and if

Brown 'adn't been and got a bit of wood and lighted the fire, and give me a drop of somethink bilin' to drink, and rubbed my legs and feet with a rough towel, I shouldn't never 'ave 'eard no more of this 'ere Rooshun marridge, and not 'ave see mornin's dawn, as the sayin' is.

So when I come to myself a bit, I says, "Why, ain't we on our way to nowheres, and ain't I been in a train along with Queen Wictorier?"

He says, "Rubbish, no."

"Well," I says, "I'll swear I 'eard a bell a-ringin' wiolent jest the same as you was a-readin' to me, as they does in Roosher when the ice is a-meltin'."

"Why," he says, "that were the Bobby a-ringin', cos I'd been and left the latch-key in the door, as I slipped on my rough coat for to go down and anser, and when I came back not a-findin' you in bed, I looked round, and found you a-settin' like a Gypshun mummy in that pail, as I suppose startled you a-comin' in suddin."

"Well," I says, "Brown, somethink must be a-goin' to 'appen to me, and I do 'ope as you'll take care of yourself when I ain't near to look arter you."

"Oh!" he says, "you'll be all right in the mornin', only you 'adn't better get up; but I'll bring you up a cup of tea, and as to goin' abroad, that ain't quite settled, and may be' shall put it off myself till the wust of the winter's over."

"Ah!" I says, "and I wish I could persuade Queen Wictorier not to go over there till spring; not but wot they'll take care of 'er, no doubt; leastways, all the care as they can, and in course they'll give the werry best of heverythink as they've got, and preaps that there Hempress of Roosher will turn out of 'er own room for 'er, but yet it won't be like 'ome; and I 'ave 'eard say as that Hemperor is that low-sperrited thro' a-livin' in constant fear of bein' sassinated, as he certingly were as near to as a toucher, by a young Pole droppin' on to 'im, close by where we was a-livin' over in Paris, that 'year as they 'ad that Exhibishun; as were all thro' 'im a-drivin' them Poles to desperashun, as in course he didn't ought to; and next time that there Pole may not miss fire so easy."

Not as he did ought to 'ave been let off, cos I do not 'old with them 'sassins, as werry oftin kills the 'rong man, the same as that party as were shot ag'in Cherrin Cross, as I forgets the name on, thro' bein' mistook for Sir Robert Peel, as is the reason I never didn't feel comfortable a-ridin' about in Paris, for fear as some of them rantypole Frenchmen should 'ave took me for a crown 'ead, and 'ad a pop at me.

So that's why I do not think as Queen Wictorier

did ought to go, let alone the cold and the things as she'll 'ave to 'ave made, as won't never come in useful, thro' bein' too warm wearin' for England.

Tho' certingly she may go over to Canader, where my Joe is, as she reigns over, some day, and then she'll want all the warm things as she've got by 'er, tho' in course she'll wear 'er royal robes over in Roosher, as is lined with fur, and so is 'er crown, as she'll find werry comfortable, if tied down under 'er chin, over 'er ears, the same as a travellin' cap, and should adwise wool in 'er royal 'ears, and a travellin' flask, with peppermint drops to suck constant, as is a fine thing when you can't get a drain, and I'm sure them Rooshuns ain't got nothink fit to drink.

"Wot do you know about the Rooshuns and their drinks?" says somebody close in my ear.

"Well," I says, "I considers that rude, but if you must know, I once 'ad a party lodge with me, as travelled in the Rooshun leather line, and were Roosher all over, down to 'is boots, as I considers a over-powerin' smell myself, tho' they do say as it will keep them moths off."

So he says, "Rubbish."

I says, "You're a gentleman."

He says, "I'm the Hemperor of all the Rooshers."

"Ah!" I says, "so my good gentleman were a-readin' me out of a book, not as I could make

out where all the Rooshers is, and," I says, "you'd
better look out for them Poles, as 'll come down on
you a cropper some day, the same as the scaffoldin'
as give way in Brick Lane, as Mrs. Challin 'adn't
passed under not more than a day afore with a
basket of manglin', as might 'ave come on 'er
only she always makes a rule of runnin', and never
won't pass under a ladder.   But," I says, "if you
will 'ave Queen Wictorier in Roosher, look out, for
if she should only take cold in 'er 'ead, parties will
say as it's foul play."

"Ah!" he says, "that's wot you all said about
Turkey, but I shall 'ave the old gobbler yet."

"Well," I says, "with all my 'art, and I don't
suppose as Queen Wictorier cares much about 'im,
so you'd better square it with her over a glass of
somethink 'ot the last thing, but don't make no
mull on it, cos of Parlyment, as ain't fond on
you."

"Oh!" he says, "Parlyment is all my eye, and
will be put down some day."

"Ah!" I says, "no doubt, and serve 'em right
too, as goes on a-jawin' and a-jawin' enuf to talk a
'orse's 'ind leg off, as the sayin' is, and yet never
don't do nothink, for I'm sure, look at Lester
Square and them Law Courts, as ain't touched, nor
yet Sunday tradin', nor your diseased wife's sister,
nor consumin' your own smoke, nor railway axci-

dence, nor yet the Beer Bill, nor the price of coals and meat and 'ouse rent, and edication, as all wants a-settin' to rights, and nothin' done."

"Ah!" he says, "if you was to 'ave me to rain over you, I'd soon settle the lot, as would give 'em a taste of the lash, cos I manages everythink myself, and don't 'ave no ministers."

"Ah!" I says, "that's werry well for a man, but 'owever could poor dear Queen Wictorier manage, as couldn't, thro' bein' a lady, go a-runnin' all over the place, and tho', in course, she do send the Prince of Wales to many places, yet it ain't the same thing as seein' 'er."

"Ah!" he says, "she'll get a lesson."

I says, "Mind as you don't play none of your tricks a-tryin' of it on with your train ile and beastliness."

"Beastliness," he says, "you jest taste it."

I says, "Never."

He says, "Nonsense, you must, and it's quite 'ot."

I says, "I should 'eave my 'art up."

He says, "Set up and drink it while it's 'ot."

I says, "Never."

He says, "Don't be a fool; here, wake up."

I says, "Nice langwidge for a Hemperor; I won't;" and I takes and turns away, as woke me up, and if I wasn't in my own bed, as 'ad dropped off agin, and Brown standin' by my side with a cup of 'ot tea, as I took, and thankful for it, and says, "'Ow I 'ave been a-dreamin'"

Says Brown, "You're a little feverish, Martha, and 'adn't better not get up jest yet."

"Oh!" I says, "I'm all right, I am."

He says, "That you ain't, and I shall send for Mr. Boltin."

I didn't say nothink, but my 'ead kep' a-runnin' on that there Rooshun marridge, and I says to myself, "I'll see Gladstin over it, tho' he do look so grim, but ain't a goin' to frighten me with 'is grim looks, and if not at 'ome," as I says to the footman as come to the door, "shall no doubt meet 'im in the street;" and sure enuf I did, jest on them steps a-goin' into the Park, as the Dook of York's Column stands on, and says to 'im, "Don't go a-'urryin' on like that; don't go a-tryin' for to dodge me, for speak to you I will."

He took 'old of my 'and quite friendly, and says, "Don't you know me? I'm Mr. Boltin."

"Well," I says, "you are somethink like 'im; but," I says, "if you're Mr. Boltin you can't be Mr. Gladstin, as is the people's William, we all knows, and, in my opinion, did ought to be ashamed on yourself to let Queen Wictorier go over there."

He says, "She ain't a-goin', only the Prince and Princess of Wales."

I says, "Don't tell me as she ain't a-goin' when I've see it in the papers, and we all knows as they don't send nothink but the truth in them telegrams."

"Why," he says, "they can't send Wictorier there by telegram."

I said, "I should 'ope not indeed, as might be blowed to atoms by them wires, as is worked by batteries, I've 'eard say, the same as the 'lectric-machine at the Pollytecknic, as nearly took my breath away, and give me the pins and needles in my 'ands up to my elbers."

"So," he says, "I'm a-goin' to a Cabinet Council, and you may as well come along."

I says, "With all my 'art, for," I says, "I'm pretty sure as Mr. Lowe is a party as will 'ear reason."

"What do you know about Lowe?" says a woice, and there he was next me; and there set Queen Wictorier and the Prince of Wales, with the Dook of Edinburrer, as I knowed in a minit thro' 'is fottygraft, not but wot he looks more pleasanter in natur than on 'is cart.

Says Queen Wictorier, a-rappin' on the table, "Order."

Says Gladstin, "I rise to order."

"Then order it quick," I says, "and let it be cool, for my mouth is that parched."

Says the Dook of Edinburrer, "Take a pull at this," jest like a sailor."

I says, "Wherever is it?"

He says, "'Ere! Why," he says, "I'm blest if Wales ain't drained it."

"Ah!" I says, "Wales is terrible things to swaller," as made somebody larf, but, law, Queen Wictorier she weren't in no chaffin' 'umour, for she says, "When you boys are quite done larfin' with Mrs. Brown, preaps you'll attend to busyness, wot we're 'ere upon;" and she says, "and you, Mrs. Brown, speak up. Do you think as this 'ere Rooshun lady can dress on fifteen pound a year, as is all her father's a-goin' to allow 'er, thro' 'avin read in a book as it can be done?"

I says, "Then all as I can say is, she must 'ave a fine set of heverythink to start with; but," I says, "dress on fifteen pound a year, why, I gives our gal ten, and she can't 'ardly keep 'erself tidy, for two or three pound a year goes in shoes, as ain't 'ardly ever off the ground."

Says Gladstin, a-puttin' in 'is oar, "Who cares about your gal?"

I says, "I do, and where you keeps but one it's a dooty."

Says Queen Wictorier, "Let Mrs. Brown 'ave 'er say."

I says, "I 'umbly thanks your grashus Majesty,

but my 'ead is that bad as I can't 'ardly 'old
it up."

Says Queen Wictorier, a-comin' close to me,
"Let me put you on these cool bandages, as is
winegar and water."

"Oh!" I says, "you'll spile your royal robes,
but you are a kind soul, tho' hevery hinch the
Queen; and," I says, "pray, wotever you do, keep
them Rooshuns under; and as to 'im a-livin' over
there, you'd better give a ewasive anser, as the
sayin' is, to that there Hemperer, and am glad for
to see as you're a-goin' to let the young couple live
in Buckenham Pallis, as'll look well; and them
Rooshuns won't know as you never lives there, and
will tickle their wanity, as the sayin' is, to think
as you've give it up to 'em; and in course its werry
well to keep up a show, partikler with Rooshuns;
and no doubt that there young Duchess will get to
speak Inglish in time, and Scotch, too, for that
matter. But," I says, "wotever is your grashus a-
drinkin'"

She says, "Nothink; it's for you as must take
it directly, the doctor says."

"Well," I says, "I don't think much of
doctor's stuff in a general way; but," I says, "this
'ere room is werry stuffy, and I feels as tho' this
'ere sofy as I'm a-layin' upon was shavin's under
me. So should like to have my bed made."

"Lay still," says Queen Wictorier.

"Well," I says, "in course I will till Gladstin and them young Princes is out of the room, tho' it does my 'art good to look at them two royal boys of yourn, thro' a rememberin' on 'em children."

Says Mrs. Padwick, as 'ad took the cup o ut of Queen Wictorier's 'and, "Come, come, Martha, take this, and don't keep on jabberin' about the Royal Family."

I says, "I tell you wot it is, I must go out this werry minit, and see Queen Wictorier at 'er own 'ouse."

"No," says Queen Wictorier, "you needn't, there's no 'urry."

I says, "I thought you wanted me to say whether them things would dye equal to new, as you ain't wore sich a time thro' constant black, not as I think they will, tho' some colours will dip better than others; and, certingly you can wear anythink over in Roosher, cos it'll be nearly all candlelight, as, in course, don't show up colours like daylight, not as a green will ever dye a good pink, in my opinion."

Gladstin he come up jest then a-glarin' all eyes, and says, "You're a-lettin' out a lot of State secrets."

I says, "I'm not the party to do it, for," I

says, "I've knowed families where they've all dressed in one another's clothes, but done that clever as would defy detection thro' not a-lettin' down tucks, but a good bit turned in at the waist, as don't show with a pania behind, tho', in course, you must 'ave a eye to growin' gals when buyin' for their sisters; but," I says, "it's a downright disgrace for to give Queen Wictorier all this bother, as did ought to 'ave all the money as she can get thro', and not be pinched for a pound or two by Parlyment; and as to that there Dilke a-darin' for to want to cut 'er down, in my opinion it's a pity as he ain't sent to Roosher, as would soon reduce 'im to a scurf, as is wot such fellers is fit for."

Says Mrs. Padwick, a-comin' close to my ear, "Now, Martha, that's a dear, try to go to sleep."

I says, "Go to sleep, and up to my eyes a-'elpin' Queen Wictorier pack; and it's a mercy as I didn't let the crown drop as I were jest a-goin' to pack in silver paper at the werry bottom of 'er box, as will be the last thing she'll want, as she won't wear it in travellin', tho,' if she'd take and tie it down over 'er ears, under 'er chin, it would be comfortable for 'er, cos the drafts is awful in railways, and any one might get a cold in their 'ead for all the crowns in the world; and they do say as old King George always wore a Welsh wig under his'n, the same as the Bishops, as would throw it into the fire in a rage if contradicted, tho' not by Queen Charlotte, as were never the woman to do it, tho' werry strict with 'er family, and died at Kew jest afore 'im."

"But," I says, "I wish as some one would give that Gladstin a bonneter, keepin' a-dancin' about the room, with my 'ead that bad and parched with thust, and do turn that Claimint ont, as I will not 'ave a-settin' up with me all night, and don't want nobody, and must get up, for there goes the bell for the train; and if that there Bob Lowe tries to 'old me down in bed, I'll scratch 'is pink eyes out; but in course, if you wishes it, Brown, I'll do my dooty, tho' it is 'ard, when I knows all about it, not to go and warn Queen Wictorier agin them Rooshuns, and don't believe as ever he'll give 'is dorter all them dimons, nor yet them millions a-year to live upon;" and then I says, "Wherever am I? In my own bed, sure enough; and there's Queen Wictorier a-settin' agin the fire, with a shawl on, a-noddin', with 'er feet on the fender; but, law," I says, "wot rubbish! I'll give a bit of a corf, and wake her up," and so I did, and up she jumps; and if it weren't Mrs. Padwick as comes to me, and says, "Oh! Martha, my dear, do you know me?"

I says, "I aint quite a idjot, thank goodness; but," I says, "I feels werry low. 'Ave I been ill?"

She says, " A little bit queer ; but," she says,
" take a drink of this."

I says, " It aint train ile, is it ? "

She says, " No, it's barley water."

I took a drink as seemed to refresh me, and felt
that weak as I didn't care to talk, so dropped off in
a quiet sleep, the quietest as I'd 'ad for many a
night ; leastways so Mrs. Padwick told me the next
day as I'd been dreadful bad, and she 'adn't 'ad 'er
clothes off for five nights ; and then Brown come
in, as I see a tear in 'is eye when he come and said,
" 'Ow are you, old gal ? "

So I says, " I must 'ave been bad ;" and Mr.
Boltin said I 'ad ; and when I were able to get up
and set in my chair, he couldn't 'elp a-smilin', and
sayin' as I would 'ave he were Gladstin and Lowe,
and sometimes the Claimint ; and as to Mrs. Padwick, she'd been Queen Wictorier, with the Prince
of Wales and the Dook of Edinburrer.

" Ah ! " I says, " it's all thro' that there Rooshun marridge, as I never could a-bear ; but, law ! "
I says, " why not ? I see thro' it all now. Why,
I'd been and got it on the brain, as the Yankees
say, cos in course the Rooshuns aint nothink to me,
and I aint one to stand in no young people's light,
I'm sure ; and if Queen Wictorier 'ad really asked
me wot I thought on it, I should 'ave said, ' It's
my opinion as parties in marryin' did ought to

please theirselves, and then if they makes a mistake, they can't blame nobody,' as is wot King
George the Fourth did used to do, I've 'eard my
dear mother say, as never could a-bear Queen
Carerline, and never took to the Princess Charlotte,
poor thing, as died with 'er fust, tho' 'ern were a
'appy marridge, and might 'ave been Queen, and 'er
children arter 'er, as would 'ave cut out Queen
Wictorier."

But I'm sure I 'ope I shan't bother my 'ead no
more about royal marridges, not when I'm light-
'eaded, for of all the nights as I 'ad, Mrs. Padwick
says, I were almost ravin', and do not feel up to
much, but shall take things quiet, so as to be well
and strong agin them 'luminations and rejoicin's as
we're a-goin' to 'ave over this weddin'; cos it
wouldn't do to let them Rooshuns think as there's
any ill-feelin's; and for my part, I'd rather 'ave
the Rooshuns than the Prooshuns, as I considers a
reg'lar set of bullies, with that old Beastmark at
their 'ead; and I'm sure it's a werry good thing
for the Rooshuns, cos if that there Hemperor of
theirn comes it too strong over 'is people, in course
Queen Wictorier, as a relation, will put in a word,
as often does good, cos tho' in course he wouldn't
stand Parlyment a-makin' them rude remarks over
money, nor yet Gladstin nor Lowe a-givin' 'im any
of their cheek, yet he might give up 'avin' of them

nobility tied up and flogged, only for jest a-differin'
with 'im, as is bein' too overbearin' even for a
Rooshun.

I'm sure I'd plenty of time to think over that
Rooshun marridge, for I don't think as ever I was
so long in gettin' about agin, and over three weeks
in my bed, as in Mr. Boltin's opinion it were the
rum as disagreed with me, tho' in general considered a 'olesome sperrit, but they do say did
ought to be a certain age afore you drank it, the
same as they gives it 'em in the navy, as is considered good for the scurvy; and I'm sure I aint
got nothink like scurvy about me; and if the rum
weren't a certain age, I'm sure I am, and don't
think as it 'ad anythink to do with it, but a 'eavy
cold, as it's lucky it come on as it did, for if I'd
started for forrin parts along with Brown, no doubt
should 'ave left my bones there.

Not as Brown went no further than Paris, thro'
a-findin' as money were not that easy to be 'ad for
no railways nor yet nothink else, thro' them French
bein' that unsettled, and don't know their own
minds, as makes me reg'lar sick and tired on 'em,
and as to a King, they wants one like the Hemperor
of Roosher, as 'll give 'em a good 'idin' now and
then; as is wot this 'ere MacMarn will do if they
don't look out, and pretty 'ot too, cos he don't look
like one to stand no nonsense, but a word and a

blow, and the blow come fust, the same as our beadle did used to when the boys would lark over the sermin.

But, law! what a place Roosher must be to be sure, as stretches all over Urope and Asher to 'Merryker; but I do 'ope as they wont want to take and show Queen Wictorier all over it, the same as Mr. Simlins did me when he took a farm out Dorkin' way, and me and Brown went to see 'im one Sunday, as would show us over everythink, from the garrets to the pig-styes; and the ladders as I went up and the steps as I come down was werry nigh the end of me, let alone a-walkin' up to my waist in a open drain, as all the stables and cow-'ouses run into, but were covered over that artful with pea-straw, as they'd been a-thrashin' in a barn and chucked outside, and I took a short cut across, never dreamin' it were all slush, and come out a mask of black filth up to my 'ips.

And that's why I never cares to go and see anyone in a new 'ouse, as is always that proud on it, and will show it you, as if anyone ever did really care about anybody's else's 'ouse; and, for my part, I do believe as there's a-many as only takes fine 'ouses jest for to come the bounce, and if they was to speak the truth would be a deal 'appier in the kitchen than in their fine parlors or drorin'-rooms.

So I was glad when Brown got back agin, and

told me all as he'd 'eard about this 'ere Rooshun
marridge, as were werry different from Miss Pilkinton's rubbish, as said as she'd 'ave dimon's the size
of a nubley coal, and as her pa wouldn't never give
'is consent unless it were promised as she should
come back whenever she pleased, and stop as long
as she liked; as aint the way to make 'er a good
wife, cos, in course, the best of friends will 'ave
their little tiffs, and if a wife can always 'ave 'er
mother and father to fly to with their complaints,
why, she aint likely to square it with 'er 'usban' not
so soon; and I do 'ope as Queen Wictorier will
put the stopper on that, as I'm sure aint the one to
incourage 'er own dorters to come 'ome a-com-
plainin', tho' they do live both close to 'er, when
she's at Win'sor or in the 'Ighlands, and might be
a-poppin' in for everlastin' with a somethink, such
as, "Oh! ma! he've been in that passion cos his
tea was smoked," or "cos he didn't like 'is dinner,"
and all manner like that.

I've been 'avin' of a good look at 'er fottygraft,
and must say as she 'ave got a pleasant sort of a
face, tho' 'er brother do look rather a bottle-nosed
party; but that may only be the way as he were
took, for I'm sure some fottygrafts is downright
effigies, as the sayin' is.

But I think this 'ere Grand Duchess, as they
calls 'er, don't seem that orful proud, nor yet one to

care about train-ile or bears'-grease, or any of them nasty ways; and as to 'er a-stickin' to 'er religion, I 'oners 'er for it; tho', in course, Queen Wictorier will 'ave all 'er grandchildren taught their Catty-kisms, as is 'er dooty thro' bein' 'ead of the Church, as must be werry puzzlin', with all them different parties a-pullin' different ways; for I'm sure there's Miss Lowtin, she's all for the Rityeralists, and it was 'er as were a-tellin' me all about that there Baldysheeno, as they won't let 'em put up; and then there's Miss Steery, she's all for Broad Church; and they both set on poor Mrs. Milkinton, as is a Misshunary's widder, and told 'er as she were out of date, a-talkin' about the elect, and procrastina-tion, as is wot Dr. Cummin' believes in, tho' es-pectin' as the world 'll soon come to a untimely end.

But, law! I espects as it will last my time, and things go on jest the same as ever; and as to Roo-sher bein' anticrust, as poor Mrs. Milkinton says 'er 'usband proved over and over agin to them savidges over in Caribee Islands, as would set on the bare rocks with nothin' on but a few feathers, a-fannin' theirselves with a plantin'-leaf, and would make as good Cristshuns for a few beads, and quite as satis-fied, as the Archbishop of Canterbury, with 'is thou-sands a-year and two pallises.

But as I said afore that there Rooshun Princess

will take the shine out of 'em all with 'er religion,
as is all picters and music, and all manner, and none of
your Scotch ways, as is what I calls a werry dismal
religion ; but as I were a-sayin' it must be 'ard
work to be the 'ead of the Church, as well as every
think else to look arter, particular in a country that
size as Roosher is ; as they do say 'ave got its eye
on Injy, but in course this 'ere marridge will stop
their games, cos in course the Dook will keep 'is
weather eye up, as the sayin' is, and he'll 'ear thro'
'is good lady if them Rooshuns is a-comin' any of
their slippery tricks, and give 'is Royal ma the
straight tip, and put her on the key weave, as the
sayin' is, and give Mr. Roosher pepper if he comes
a-'ankerin' arter Injier.

Cos in course if he didn't, he'd be a traitor, and
get shot like that there Marshal Bazeen were not,
tho' wot he were let off for nobody knows, arter
bein' found guilty by all them counts, as was
always agreed, and in course did ought to 'ave
been shot the same as Marshal Nay, cos, as I says,
if you can't trust a sojer or a perliceman, whoever
are you to trust, the same as poor Mrs. Cortle,
as were robbed of 'er six silver tea-spoons by a
airey sneak, and a feller come to the door that
werry afternoon as I were a-settin' with 'er, and
says he were a detective, and asks 'er if she's got
any more tea-spoons like 'em.

She says, " Oh ! yes, the other six as makes up the dozen."

" Then," he says, " give 'em me."

She says, " Wot for ? "

" Why," he says, "we've got the boy, and want your other spoons to indemnify them by, as he 'ad took."

She says to me, " Shall I give 'em 'im ? "

I says " Is he a detective ? "

She says, " Not a-knowin' cannot say," but she goes to the cupboard, and gets out the other six tea-spoons, and says, " he looks respectable."

I says, " Does he ? " for I 'adn't seen 'him thro' a-stoppin' in the passage, as I didn't think looked well.

It were jest a-gettin' dusk, and I went to the winder jest as she were a-givin' 'im the spoons, and see a perliceman at the gate.

So I taps at the winder and beckons 'im up to to the door jest as that feller were a-goin' to step out at it with the spoons.

He started back when he see the perlice, and I got to the door by that time, a-sayin' to Mrs. Cortle " You'd better 'ave a witness as you give the spoons, so I called up this perliceman," as dropped onto that detective, as he called 'isself, like a knife, as the sayin' is, and collared 'im, spoons and all ; but, law, I didn't get no thanks but only trouble for my

pains; and as to Mrs. Cortle, she were in 'er bed
for weeks with roomatics, after 'angin' about that
Sessions to persecute that willin', as were a reglar
thief, but only got six months, as he jeered at the
ideer on, and said as he'd be even with that old
sack of fat, illudin' to me; as made the Judge tell
'im if he laid a finger on me he'd give 'im five year;
but wot good would that do me, with my jaw
broke or maimed for life.

And I must say as I'm glad as it aint a French
Princess as the Dook's goin' to marry, cos they are
that dreadful unsettled; and whyever don't they
stick to a thing when they say it, and shoot that
Bazeen or else let 'im go Scotch free, as the sayin' is.

As to 'is wife, she's only a nigger or somethink
like that, so in course she wouldn't mind 'is bein'
'anged, drored, and quartered, as is wot she used
to over there, cos I 'ave 'eard say as them Mexikins
is the biggest savages out.

Mrs. Padwick, she've got a book as is full of
them old sayin's, and one of them is old Bonyparty,
as said the Rooshuns will be our masters some day.

Then, I says, "It's a good match as Queen Wictorier 'ave made for 'er son, cos he'll be the right
side when the row comes, and put in a good word
for 'is family, not," I says, "as I'm afeared of all
the Rooshuns as ever was born, so long as they don't
force me to eat that there cavyar, for of all the fishy

ile as ever I did taste, it's the wust, tho' some likes to eat it on their bread, like jam, but they do say is 'olesome for them Rooshuns, jest the same as them parties in them Poler bear regions eats all the inside of a whale, as keeps 'em from a-freezin' up.

And that's why I don't believe as Queen Wictorier will go all that way, as, no doubt, 'ave 'ad a werry perlite inwitation with the Hemperor of all the Rooshers, a-presentin' of 'is dooty to Queen Wictorier, and 'opes as she'll make one at my dorter's weddin' with 'er son; as no doubt would rite back as Queen Wictorier 'ave the 'oner to acquaint the Hemperor as I goes out that seldom, and always in black, as would throw a gloom over a weddin', let alone the fateeg, as can't be got at in a night, like Scotland, and yet would feel a pleasure like in a-witnessin' of my son's 'appiness with your dorter, as may be werry sure as Queen Wictorier will receive 'er with hopin' harms on board of my own yott, with all the yards manned, and "Rule Britannier" all over the place, as is a Inglishman's glory, like Lord Nelson in the harms of "Wictory" at Spithead, and went down like the "Royal George," without a murmur, and the ports all open, as is why I never did 'old with Free Trade, as 'ave been the ruin of Old Ingland you may depend, and don't ketch forriners like the 'Merrykins sich fools as to

give into it, and as to Rooshuns, there's nothink
free about them any more than the 'Merrykins, as
took and give them down South a reglar woppin'
the moment they begun to talk about bein' let go
free, not but wot the South give the North a
doosed good thrashin' afore they could get the
upper 'and, not but wot I 'olds with some one
a-bein' master, and not goin' on that foolish like
they will in France, 'avin' fust one and then another to rule over 'em, and I do 'ope as this 'ere
MacMarn will take and give 'em the soundest
thrashin' as ever they 'ad, if they comes any of their
Red Republickin ways, not but wot there's werry
respectable publickins as keeps decent 'ouses, but
that's no reason as they should try for to come a-
rulin' over other people as aint in the public line,
and a-burnin' of places with pitroleum, as is worse
than murder, as always will come out, as the sayin'
is, but water itself won't put out that wile pitroleum,
as nobody else but devils would think of usin' agin
their fellow-creeturs; but, I says, in my opinion,
mobs ain't no better than devils broke loose, as is
the reason as it's better to read the Riot Act, and
fire on 'em at once, cos showin' of 'em mercy only
is a-doin' a injury to innercent bein's, as is werry
often shot by mistake in the 'urry of the moment,
not as ever you ketches me out in a row, as won't
go over the door, even Guy Fox night, as is shame-

ful riots, and reglar Bedlam broke loose at Lewes, as the roughs makes a reglar stand-up fight on it.

I do 'ope as there won't be no rows over the 'luminations for this 'ere Royal marridge, as I 'ears is to be werry grand in Scotland, but I'm sure if they goes a-lightin' up that old town of Edinburrer, they'll soon set it all in a blaze, as is a ramshackle old place, and some of them narrer alleys would be jest as well burnt down, only but for the poor as lives in 'em, as loves their 'omes, 'owever 'umble, 'cos, as the sayin' is, "be it never so lowly, there's no place like 'ome," tho' it's up five pair of stairs.

Miss Pilkinton, she's quite a-takin' on over this 'ere Rooshun marridge, cos she's been told as all the royal family is a-goin' over there to it, and she thinks as there's some conspiracy for to take 'em all out in a boat for a pleasurin' and then knock a 'ole in 'er bottom, and drown the lot, and then the Rooshuns would get old Ingland under their thumb.

I says, "Go along with your rubbish. Why, 'owever could they take 'em out in a boat, when it's all froze over, and do you think as that there Duke of Edinburrer would stand by and see 'is ma, and all 'is royal family bein' drownded?"

"Ah!" she says, "he'd be drugged, in course, and if it is all froze, wot's to perwent 'em from a-takin' of 'em over a part as is dangerous, and gettin' 'em all into a 'ole?"

I says, "Queen Wictorier were not born yesterday, as the sayin' is, and aint quite so green as to
go a-trustin' of 'er royal weight where the ice is
'rote up dangerous; besides," I says, "do you
think as the Prince of Wales is such a green'orn as
that?"

"No," I says, "there's no fear escept their
takin' cold, thro' a-wearin' low dresses at the
weddin' or anythink like that, the same as Miss
Amber, as is over sixty, and a reglar prize bullock
for fat, as went to 'er own niece's weddin' in a
book muslin' for a bridesmaid, as she'd 'ad by 'er
for years, with a new body as didn't match, and
white boots, as turned out a pourin' day, and got
'er feet sopped thro', with a cab as leaked at the
bottom, as she set in all the arternoon, cos she
thought they set off 'er foot, with roomattic fever,
as werry nigh settled 'er 'ash, as the sayin' is, and
no doubt all them bridesmaids over there, will 'ave
their things lined with flannin and cork soles inside their boots, tho' injy rubber overshoes is the
safest, but don't do in a French railway with them
'ot water things for your feet, as will melt them to
a jelly, the same as gutter-percher soles, as is
things I never could a-bear, and melted right off
my feet, thro' a-puttin' 'em up on the fender, jest
to warm, and stuck to the 'arth-rug when I went
to walk, so reglar put my foot in it, as the sayin'

is, and 'ad to go 'ome in a cab in a pair of Mrs.
Padwick's list shoes, as was the only thing I could
get over my instep, thro' it bein' that arch as
always makes 'em as fits me with my shoes stare
agin; and one time, as I tried to get a pair of boots
over in Paris, the young man said to the lady of the
shop, "Oh ! that colosse," as is Latin for anythink
as is remarkable fine. So I knows as I've got a foot
as anyone might be proud on, and knows 'ow to
put it down firm when I've made up my mind, as
led to that row in the bus with the old feller as 'ad
got 'is shoes all cut for the gout, as in course I
couldn't see in the dark down among the straw, as
no doubt were painful, but needn't 'ave felled me
back'ards like a ox, as sent the two as was a-gettin'
in arter me flyin' out agin, and my umbreller 'andle
across the bridge of the gent's nose a-settin' oppersite 'im, as led to 'im a-givin' me in charge,
leastways, tried to, only the Bobby didn't see it.

"But," as I says to Mrs. Padwick, "it is downright rubbish for Miss Pilkinton to run down them
Rooshuns, as is a 'ardy lot, and in course would
shoot our Sailor Prince down to the ground, as the
sayin' is, and it's a good thing as he's a-goin' to
settle down, cos we all knows wot a light-arted lot
sailors is, when they comes ashore, a-flingin' of
their money about right and left all over the place,
and no doubt Queen Wictorier would let 'im 'ave 'is

fling for a bit, and then, like a true mother, would
pull 'im up, a-sayin' 'My dear Halfred, you must
not go a-spendin' of your money like this all your
life, tho' I likes to see you that liberal, as is your
natur', not as I considers Parlyment 'ave been over
free with the money, but, never mind, there'll be a
somethink for all on you, some day, Parlyment or no
Parlyment, as no doubt she considers a mean lot,
and 'ow should they know wot Princes wants, and
wot'll keep 'em respectable, and 'ave showed wot
she thinks, by a-givin' up 'er own pallis to the
young couple, so as they mayn't cut a mean figger
afore the Rooshuns as comes over along with 'er."

I could 'ave jumped for joy, as the sayin' is,
when I 'eard as Queen Wictorier were not a-goin'
to Roosher, but sent 'er love to the Hemperor, a-
sayin' as she 'oped to come when the days gets
longer; but, in my opinion, they'll be long enuf
afore they ketches 'er a-trustin' of 'erself to all that
hice and snow, partikler as we're a-'avin' sich a mild
winter 'ere—leastways, we mustn't 'oller till we're
out of the wood, as the sayin' is; and I'm sure we
shall be out of wood and coals too in another week,
but the 'ardest frost ever knowed set in arter Feb-
ruary 'ad begun, and, if it should do, will make
that young Rooshun Princess feel more at home; as
I do 'ope they'll keep up good fires in Buckin'am
Pallis, as must want airin', partikler the beds, as

will draw the damp if not slep' in.   Not but wot it
must put Queen Wictorier in a bit of a fidget
lettin' that son of 'ern go alone, tho' in course the
others didn't seem to see a-goin', partikler the
Prince of Wales, as is that fond of the children as
he won't 'ave 'is breakfast without 'em, as would
'ave been a great risk to take 'em to Roosher.   Tho'
I'm sure we mustn't talk, arter them fogs as killed
so many a-gettin' down their throats, like the prize
beasts at the Cattle Show, as can't never 'ardly
draw their breaths for fat; the same as Mrs. Pul-
turer, as never laid down for years afore she died,
and shook the floor with 'er breathin'.   So it's all
off my mind now, and no doubt Queen Wictorier see
to all Alfred' under-clothin', and made 'im promise
solemn as he'd wear 'is wusted socks, with wot the
French call "a catch-nay" round 'is throat; for I
'ave 'eard say as Berling's as cold as Roosher, and
he didn't ought to 'ave gone to see that hold Hemperor with a bad cold on 'is chest, as is werry
ketchin', and wouldn't never do to 'ave 'im go to be
married with the mumps, or even a swelled face
as is werry disfiggerin', and don't look well in a
bridegroom to 'ave a bit of flannin round your face
at the halter, tho' I 'ave knowed parties as went to
church on crutches, rather than 'ave it put off, cos
there's many a slip, partikler in Roosher; and I do
'ope as he'll think to 'ave a bit of list round 'is

10

shoes when a-walkin' on the hice; cos, tho' it don't
look dressy, it's better than breakin' a limb, or even
puttin' your elber out, as would be orkard to put
on the ring with your left 'and, or even your arm in
a sling. As is 'ow that feller managed to pick my
pocket in the omblebus, as were all make-believe,
and no more broken than mine, or else couldn't
never 'ave got my port-money out of my pocket,
and put it back agin empty, as was over fifteen
shillin's in it. No doubt, there's 'igh jinks over in
Roosher, as I should like to see, but must read all
about it in the papers, as 'll 'ave picters of it, as,
no doubt, will be jest the same as all them Royal
doin's; and well remembers Queen Wictorier bein'
married 'erself jest like yesterday, as the sayin' is;
and shan't never forget the 'luminations in a coal-
waggon, as we was in over eleven 'ours, thro' bein'
stuck over five in back streets, where there wasn't
nothink to be seen but the yells of the mobs, as
kep' a-passin' with fieldmales a-shriekin', and poor
Mrs. Baggerly, as 'ad nearly all 'er clothes tore off
'er back jest agin Cherrin' Cross, but no lives lost
as ever I 'eard on; tho', in course, them as was
fools enuf to go out with anythink in their pockets
never took it 'ome agin; and poor Jane Toomey 'ad
nearly all 'er back-'air tore out by the roots thro' it
a-comin' down under 'er bonnet, and a-gettin' of it
tangled in a party's umbreller-'andle, as were a

foolish thing to bring out to see 'luminations with; as aint like a telescope for to look at the moon with, the same as I did one night in Lester Square, and were reglar 'ustled and robbed by a lot of wagger-bones of both sects as come round me.

But, as I were a-sayin', we must put on a good face for to receive this 'ere Grand Duchess, so I means to 'ave my welwet jacket steamed as good as new, with a broad gimp round it, and were a-goin' to 'ave fur round the cuffs and collars, only, as I were a-sayin' to Mrs. Padwick, parties will say as I'm a-dressin at Queen Wictorier in her last fotty-graft without 'er weeds, as shows 'er sense, cos it don't do to go on a-grievin' for ever, leastways not outward, as is wot weeds means, though I'm sure Mrs. Pendleton, at the " Coach and 'Orses," was as full of 'er fun within a week, tho' weeds and lappets a-flyin' and crape up to 'er waist. I shan't 'ave no flowers in my bonnet, thro' 'avin' a Marryboo feather, as is crimson, and goes well with green satting. I've got one of them quilted pettycoats, as is all stripes, and my pollernaise is a puce with yaller spots over it, as will look dressy, tho' not conspickuous; tho' I shouldn't wonder if I did ketch the young couple's heye on the curb-stone, a-waitin' for them to pass; not but wot I shall see 'em closer, no doubt, for I've 'eard say as that Dook of Edinburrer, 'ave 'eard speak on me thro'

some low-lived feller a-takin' of me off afore 'im;
and all the royal family knows about me, as is werry
fond on me, thro' well a-knowin' as I'm a real
friend; and though I'd tell 'em the truth, yet I'd
scorn to give in to any of them lies about 'em, and
'ave give parties a good settin' down as 'ave spoke
disrespectful on any of 'em; and as to Queen Wictorier, I've 'ad a 'int as when she comes to stop in
town agin reglar, I'm a-goin' to be appinted one of
them back-stairs parties, as is called women, but is
ladies, and 'onerable ladies too, all the time; not as
ever I shall be one to care to 'ave my name in the
papers as 'avin' the 'oner of dinin' with 'er Majesty,
as shall always 'ave my cup of tea along with 'er
early, cos Brown won't never stand me a-bein' kep'
late at nights; so, when I've see 'er royal bed
turned down, I shall jest 'ook it 'ome, as can get a
bus at the Wictoria Station as will get me 'ome
under the 'arf hour, and will keep a place for me if
a reg'lar customer, and set me down at Buckin'am
Pallis, thro' a-passin' by the back gate, as is Gros-
venor Place. Not as it would be any good me
a-bein' there for to receive this 'ere young bride,
thro' not a-speakin' no Rooshun, but a dab at
French, thro' a-studyin' of it without a master, as
you can learn like 'ritin' in six lessons; but I do
'ope as I may be useful in nussin', cos though I
aint got a word to say agin Mrs. Williams nor the

other lady as nussed the Prince of Wales, yet in
course Queen Wictorier would be more easy in 'er
mind if she knowed as I were there, and so would
the Hempress of Roosher, cos, tho' no doubt she'd
come, yet couldn't be no use thro' not a-under-
standin' a word as was said, but must learn myself
wot the Rooshun is for gruel, and a rushlight,
and all them other things as a lady might require; cos it's all werry fine, but there aint
nothink like a rushlight arter all for a sick room,
thro' not a-givin' no glare, nor yet a-throwin'
out no 'eat, not as it's a cheerful light, partikler
with them 'oles in the rushlight shade a-showin' on
the wall, but then you don't want nothink exciting
in a sick room, as did ought to be kep' quiet; and
as to gruel, the givin' on it up 'ave proved fatal to
a many as I've knowed, thro' bein' put too for'ard.
Not as I'm a-goin' in for nussin' at my time of life,
but shall be proud and 'appy for to give my adwice
as 'ave 'ad doctors quail afore me, when the patient
were dangerous, as am one myself, as 'olds with
natur' takin' of its course. But as to ladies a-turnin'
nusses, as knows nothink about it, why, it's wuss
than murder, tho' in course they means well, the
same as they did over in the Crimeer; but all as
I've got to say is, as they shouldn't nuss me. But,
law, as Brown would say, 'ow I am a-runnin' on,
a-lookin' into footurity, as the sayin' is. And I do

'ope as that there dear young Prince Arthur will be
the next, and blessed with the gal of 'is 'art, as no
doubt, like all them sojer boys, he'vo left behind
'im somewheres, as 'is nice 'ansom face would make
many a 'art 'eavy at partin' with 'im. And it's my
best wishes as Queen Wictorier may live for to see
'em all married and settled, as 'ave too much sense
to spile 'er grandchildren, tho' no doubt, jest like
me, she lets 'em 'ave their own way more than ever
sho did their royal pas and mas when they was
little, as is the way of the world; and in my
opinion it's cos grandchildren is more like play-
things than your own ever was, and don't feel it
the same dooty for to correct 'em, nor yet check
'em when a-goin' too far with the cake, or a
drinkin' with their mouth full, or a-goin' in 'eavy
for toffee, or gettin' too rude in their romps. But
whether it's marridges or christenin's, I'm sure I'm
always 'appy and proud for to serve Queen Wictorier as I looks on as a mother as the sayin' is,
tho' in course there is five years atween us, as
couldn't be mother and dorter, not in the course of
natur, as the sayin' is.

Says Mrs. Padwick, " I should like to see them
presents, as they're a-goin' to 'ave."

" Yes," I says, " and that one from all the fleet,
as will be a size, if every man's a-goin' to give 'em
somethink, includin' the marines, as is all the

fashion now to 'ave odd plates, and cups and saucers, and no doubt the poorest will give a some-think, like a true British tar, and you may be sure as that there Sailor Prince, he'll fancy the poorest best, as is like 'is Royal ma, bless 'er 'art, and he'll be a-drinkin' out of a 'umble willer pattern, when others is a-gorgin' theirselves off gold, and would be wexed if them poor fellers went a-pinchin' of theirselves and their families to give 'im 'andsome things jest to show 'ow they loves 'im, as will 'ave to ask 'em all to tea and supper, cos a dinner would come too 'eavy on a young married couple, as wouldn't feel a cup of tea, and somethink genteel in the way of tripe and sprats for supper, with a bit of cold beef and a meat pie on the side table, cos sailors 'as appetites, we all knows, and in course wouldn't espect nothink but beer, and grog, with their pipes when the ladies 'as left the room."

I do 'ope they won't get a-dancin' none of them 'ornpipes, for I don't believe as them floors will stand it, as aint like between-decks, as if you do go thro' there's only the oshun to fall on, as in course a sailor's at much at 'ome in as 'is own hammocks.

Not but wot some would give the world to 'ave a bit of a dance with the Dook, a-standin' on a tub a-fiddlin' to 'em that afferble, as no doubt he 'ave done scores of times of a Saturday night at sea,

like a reglar sailor, a-toastin' of sweethearts and
wives, and plays the fiddle like a angel, I've 'eard
say, as is reglar mad arter music, and will go
anywheres to 'ear it, and will ketch a fiddle out of
one of their 'ands at the theayter, and scrape away
with the best on 'em; not, in course, as he'd take
it up reglar, cos that would be a-takin' of the
bread out of poor men's mouths, as the sayin' is.

I certingly do mean to 'ave a party myself on
the weddin' day, and shall 'ave young Roberts and
'is wife, as 'ave played the fiddle by 'is ears from
the cradle; and if we don't 'ave a dance and a
bowl of punch, it shan't be my fault, as aint forgot
my steps not altogether, and remembers shassy,
croisy, and pusset, quite well.

Cos in my opinion we did all ought to show
them Rooshuns as we've been and done 'em a 'oner,
and as money aint no objec.

But I do 'ope as she won't want to be always
talkin' Rooshun, cos of the children, as it would
'urt Queen Wictorier's feelin's for to 'ave a lot of
little Rooshun bears for grandchildren, as she
couldn't make out wot they wanted, the same as
poor Mrs. Amber's dorter, as went over there and
married a party as lived in Pest, and come 'ome a
widder with nine little Pests, as was the plague of
'er life, and couldn't speak nothink but gibberish
as nobody couldn't make out, but understood me

when I took the broom-'andle to 'em when I ketched 'em a-torturin' of a cat, the young beasts; and that's wot Queen Wictorier did ought to do, as don't look like a-thinkin' of correctin' 'em, before-'and, if you jest ketches up the 'arth-broom as is 'angin' on a nail by the fireside, and give 'em a tap when they don't mind a word as you says.

Cos it's all rubbish a-escusin' on 'em a-sayin' as they don't understand, cos all children knows when they're a-doin' 'rong, whether forriners or not, from niggers upwards, even down to the dog, as'll crouch when he've been a-doin' 'rong, afore you've found it out; and as to our cat, I'm sure when he broke my large puddin'-basin, why, he 'id 'isself for three days in the coals, tho' I'd never believe as he went to do it, but all that gal's fault a-leavin' it on the hedge of the washus winder.

But yet, for all that, I shouldn't fancy a lot of forrin grandchildren, so 'opes as Queen Wictorier won't 'ave that trial for 'er old age, tho', bless 'er, she's in 'er prime still, thro' a-marryin' that young 'erself, as seems only like a year or two ago, tho' in course, sight of them princes makes one think 'ow time flies, as the sayin' is.

So, on the 'ole, I thinks as this 'ere Rooshin marridge is a good thing, and preaps some of these fine days Ingland and Roosher will be all one, as'll make pretty near all the world one, cos in course

them Merrykins will come to 'avin' kings and
queens like other people, when they comes to 'ave
the sense to see wot a 'umbug it is to 'ave a Presi-
dent as'll some day take and punch their 'eads all
round when he gets strong enuf to do it, as is jest
wot they all do when once they gets in, like a
Member of Parlyment, as will promise anythink
when a-askin' for your wote, and then, when once
he've got in, will take a sight at you, as the sayin'
is, and see you blowed fust afore he'll do anythink
for you.

That's why I 'oners that there Count Shambore,
as aint no sham at all, but a real king, and won't
stoop to no dirty lyin' ways to get 'is crown, as is
'is rights, but speaks out like a man; and as to 'is
stickin' to 'is flag, why, I likes a man as sticks to
'is colours, as is wot Brown says did ought to be
every Inglishman's glory; and as he were a-sayin'
to a party we knows as arf French thro' the father's
side, "Why," he says, "wotever 'ave you French
got to be proud on, with that there beastly tree-
colour, as aint the tree-colour of liberty, as was set
up by a murderin' lot of roughs and willins, and
stained with innercent blood, and were the cuss of
Europe when old Boney went a-robbin' and a-mur-
derin' all over the world, as didn't bring you much
glory in Roosher, nor yet at Waterloo, under the
old man; and when that other feller went out with it

for to fight them Germins, he didn't get much glory at Sedan, with all 'is tree-colour ; but he's dead and gone, so let 'im rest, and let's 'ope 'is name wont be the cause of no more blood and murder in the world, but as we may 'ave a lastin' peace, as no doubt these 'ere marridges will lead to.

These were Brown's sentiments, as I agrees to, and I'm sure so will Queen Wictorier, and if that Rooshun Hemperor don't like 'em, why, he'd better not come 'ere a-botherin' us ; tho', in my opinion, 'is father were hevery inch a king, as I see 'im that time he came to London on the quiet like, and come along the Dover Road, a-'ead and shoulders taller than all the rest.

Not as them tall people always turns out the best ; for there was young Oplins, as were in the Life Guards, and sold out to marry old Carrins' dorter, he went off at the knees, and turned out to 'ave two wives already, as he got five year for, and serve 'im right, a willin, as did used to come a-swaggerin' down our street as big as bull beef, in spurs, and quite different to them Royal Princes as is that nice and quiet in their ways, and don't give theirselves no hairs, always a-studyin' to please their Royal ma, as 'ave set 'em that good esample, as werry few is like 'er ; and I'm sure it's a mussy as Queen Lizzybeth never 'adn't no family, leastways, to be Queen arter 'er, for a nice nest of wipers we

should 'ave 'ad to rain over us, and for my part I
aint got no fears about them Rooshuns adoin'
Queen Wictorier any 'arm, as is not likely to foller
no bad esamples, well a-knowin' as Brittins never,
never, never shall be slaves, as is wot her sailor
son is always a-singin' to 'er, and will no doubt 'ave
often sung to them Rooshuns, when asked for a
song arter supper, at one of them family parties
as must want cheerin' up a bit, and there aint
a place where Rule Britannier sounds more nat'ral
to a Rooshun year, cos they knows the tune;
and it's as well as they should be reminded on
it now and then, and that's no doubt why the
Dook of Edinburrer now and then tips 'em a
stave on it, at the sayin' is, when they took 'im
a-sailin' about in that there beastly Black Sea, as
were the loss of thousans to us; I don't mean money,
but dear, brave ones, Inglish boys as fell like men,
and 'ave see their monyments jest by Westminster
Abbey, and made the tears come in my eyes, the
same as every Inglish mother must feel, and 'ave
'eard say as Queen Wictorier took and busted into
tears 'erself, when she got the letter about that
there Inkerman, where they fell.

So no doubt the Dook 'as got the straight tip
from 'is Royal ma, when they come the bounce a-sailin'
there agin, as much as to say, "We don't care a
blow about Ingland a-sayin' as we was to keep out

of the Black Sea ;" why he no doubt took and struck up "Rule Britannier" on 'is wiolin, as gave them Rooshuns a turn no doubt; for in course he's true Britannier metal, and tho' he may 'ave fell in love with one of them Rooshuns, it don't prove as he 'olds with all their ways, nor yet a-goin' to knock under to 'em, any more than young Miles as fell in love with one of them nigger gals, as 'er father called 'isself a king, and got 'er to run away with 'im, but took precious good care to rob the old man of all but wot he stood upright in, as were only a rush mat and a red feather, as weren't worth takin', but all the ready money as he 'ad, as was mostly shells and a war club; not as I considered she were a-doin' 'er dooty; but, law, that were a many years ago, jest arter Prince Le Boo, tho' my grandmother remembered 'er well, as were as black as lead, and never fancied 'er thro' a-likin' raw meat.

But in course Rooshuns is werry different, and in course we don't bear no mallis about that Crimeer, and shall all be the best of friends, and live to see the Rooshuns jest at much at 'ome 'ere as the Germans 'as made theirselves.

Simmons & Botten, Printers, Shoe Lane, London, E.C.

NOVELS AT ONE SHILLING.

(*Postage* 3d.)

BY CAPTAIN MARRYAT.

Peter Simple.
The King's Own.
Midshipman Easy.
Rattlin the Reefer.
The Pacha of Many
Tales.

Newton Forster.
Jacob Faithful.
Japhet in Search of a
Father.
The Dog-Fiend.
The Poacher.

The Phantom Ship.
Percival Keene.
Valerie.
Frank Mildmay.
Olla Podrida.
Monsieur Violet.

BY J. FENIMORE COOPER.

The Last of the Mo-
hicans.
The Spy.
Lionel Lincoln.
The Deerslayer.
The Pathfinder.
The Bravo.

The Waterwitch.
The Two Admirals.
The Red Rover.
Satanstoe.
Afloat and Ashore.
Wyandotte.
The Headsman.

Homeward Bound.
The Sea Lions.
Precaution.
Mark's Reef.
Ned Myers.
The Heidenmauer.

BY G. P. R. JAMES.

Agincourt.
Attila.
Margaret Graham.
Delaware.

Henry of Guise.
Dark Scenes.
The Smuggler.
Rose D'Albret.

John Marston Hall.
Beauchamp.
Arrah Neil.
My Aunt Pontypool.

BY ALEXANDRE DUMAS.

The Three Musketeers.
Twenty Years After.
Doctor Basilius.
The Twin Captains.
Captain Paul.
Memoirs of a Physician.   2 vols.
The Queen's Necklace.
The Chevalier de Maison Rouge.
The Countess de Charny.

Monte Cristo.   2 vols.
Nanon ; or, Woman's War.
The Two Dianas.
The Black Tulip.
The Forty-Five Guardsmen.
Taking the Bastille.   2 vols.
Chicot the Jester.
The Conspirators.
Ascanio.

BY W. H. AINSWORTH.

Windsor Castle.
Tower of London.
The Miser's Daughter.
Rookwood.
Old St. Paul's.
Crichton.

Guy Fawkes.
The Spendthrift.
James the Second.
The Star Chamber.
The Flitch of Bacon.
Mervyn Clitheroe.

Lancashire Witches.
Ovingdean Grange.
St. James's.
Auriol.
Jack Sheppard.

Published by George Routledge and Sons.

Novels at One Shilling.—*Continued.*

BY VARIOUS AUTHORS.

Violet the Danseuse.
The Royal Favourite. *Mrs. Gore.*
Joe Wilson's Ghost. *Banim.*
Ambassador's Wife. *Mrs. Gore.*
The Old Commodore.
Author of "Rattlin the Reefer."
Cinq Mars. *De Vigny.*
Ladder of Life. *A. B. Edwards.*
My Brother's Keeper.
Miss Wetherell.
The Scarlet Letter. *Hawthorne.*
Respectable Sinners.
The House of the Seven Gables.
Hawthorne.
Whom to Marry. *Mayhew.*
Henpecked Husband. *Lady Scott.*
The Family Feud. *Thos. Cooper.*
Nothing but Money.
T. S. Arthur.
Letter-Bag of the Great Western.
Sam Slick.
Moods. *Louisa M. Alcott.*
Singleton Fontenoy. *J. Hannay.*
Kindness in Women.
Mohegan Maiden, and other Tales
Stories of Waterloo.

Zingra the Gipsy.
My Brother's Wife.
Tom Jones.
The Duke.
My Cousin Nicholas. [sion.
Northanger Abbey, and Persua-
Land and Sea Tales.
The Warlock.
Echoes from the Backwoods.
Baithazar. *Balzac.*
Eugenie Grandet.
The Vicar of Wakefield.
The Sparrowgrass Papers.
A Seaside Sensation. *C. Ross.*
A Week with Mossoo. *Chas. Ross.*
Miss Tomkins' Intended.
Arthur Sketchley.
On the Road. *B. Hemyng.*
A Bundle of Crowquills.
The Hidden Path.
A Sailor's Adventures.
The Medical Student. *A. Smith.*
Love Tales. *G. H. Kingsley.*
The Backwoods Bride.
Kent the Ranger.
Ennui. *Edgeworth.*

BEADLE'S LIBRARY.
Price 6d. each. (Postage 1d.)

Alice Wilde.
The Frontier Angel.
Malaeska.
Uncle Ezekiel.
Massasoit's Daughter.
Bill Biddon, Trapper.
Backwoods Bride.
Sybil Chase.
Monowano, the Shaw-
nee Spy.
Brethren of the Coast.
King Barnaby.
The Forest Spy.
The Far West.
Riflemen of Miami.
Alicia Newcombe.
The Hunter's Cabin.

The Block House.
Esther ; or, The Ore-
gon Trail.
The Gold Hunters.
Mabel Meredith.
The Scout.
The King's Man.
Kent the Ranger.
The Peon Prince.
Laughing Eyes.
Mahaska, the Indian
Queen.
The Slave Sculptor.
Myrtle.
Indian Jem.
The Wrecker's Bride.
The Cave Child.

The Lost Trail.
Joe Davis's Client.
The Cuban Heiress.
The Hunter's Escape.
The Silver Bugle.
Pomfret's Ward.
Quindaro.
The Rival Scouts.
On the Plains.
Star Eyes.
The Mad Skipper.
Little Moccasin.
The Doomed Hunter.
Eph. Peters.
The Fugitives.
Big-Foot the Guide.

Published by George Routledge and Sons.